Dope Boy

Fetish

A Hood Love Story

By Shacarra

D1368315

D1415929

Published by Shani Greene-Dowdell Presents

Subsidiary of Nayberry Publications/TBRS Newprint

www.nayberrypublications.com

Opelika, Alabama, 36801, USA

Cover Art by TSPubcreative.

Printed in the United States of America

PUBLISHER'S NOTE

This is a work of fiction. Names, characters, places, and incidents either are the product of the author's imagination or are used fictitiously, and any resemblance to actual persons, living or dead, business establishments, events, or locales is entirely coincidental.

The publisher does not have any control over and does not assume any responsibility for author or third-party Web sites or their content.

NEWSLETTER SIGNUP

Thanks for your support! To receive future updates from Shani Greene-Dowdell Presents, text NAYBERRY to 22828.

DEDICATION

This book is dedicated to everyone who helped me along the way.

Prologue

I can feel my heart pounding in my chest as my breath becomes shorter. Sweat is pouring down my face soaking my shirt, and my pants are hanging off my ass. This motherfucker tried to set me up. Now his whole gang of boys are firing shots and wanting me dead. I start to feel a burning sensation throughout my chest. I am almost out of breath. My body wants to stop, but my mind thinks the opposite. I have to make it to my hood, at least. I run until I pass the old auto shop that Mr. Sims used to own.

I smoke too much weed.

I am thirteen, and I can't even run like normal kids my age. I bend over to tie my sneakers and catch my breath. Fifteen minutes pass by, and I can finally breathe normally again. I rage with anger as I walk home, thinking about how I could get revenge on this nigga. Nobody sets me up and gets away with it.

When I reach the crib, I find my brother, Terrell, sitting on the porch staring off into space. *Shit.* He must be in one of his moods, which has become the norm for him. Grandma must've set him off again. The same routine happens almost three times a week. My grandma tells him how sorry he is and how he needs to get his life together because she isn't gonna tolerate his bullshit anymore. Then she adds, "Your lil' bad-ass brother too!" My brother and I rarely receive any love from our folks. That's why we've become so close.

When I walk up the steps to the porch, Terrell snaps out of his thoughts and looks at me with concern on his face.

"Damn lil' bro. What the hell happened to you?" he asks.

Quickly, I grab a seat on the old dusty-ass couch my folks never wanted to get rid of. They had this couch since the 1950's when they moved into their first apartment. I swipe the sweat off my face.

"Well," Terrell says, "What happened to you?"

I shake my head. "Brah, Que tried to set me up."

Terrell sits up from the porch rail, and his body stiffens.

"What you mean?"

"Nigga set his boys up to rob and kill me. I swear if I didn't listen to my gut feeling, I would've been dead!"

Terrell frowns and begins to pace back and forth.

"Were you strapped?" he asks.

I shake my head and answer, "No."

"I'll be damned if I let this fool get away with this shit. He can't get away with this!" Terrell says with emphasis on *can't*.

"Sholl can't," I chime in.

"We gon' get his ass lil' bro! And that's on my life!"

And indeed we mean that shit. We go on the search for Que for three days straight. We make sure to stay low, but we have connections and, finally, one of our woes passes along some valuable information. *Got 'em.*

On May third around midnight, my life changes forever. Terrell and I hide in an unmarked car and wait for Que to come outside of the hole in the wall. As soon as I see his monkey ass exit the building behind the alleyway, my chest fills with rage. My brother starts running down the plan.

"Now remember bro, we're just going to scare him. Fuck him up a lil. You hea—"

I hop out the car without listening to the rest of my brother's plan. I run fast as I make my way to Que. I hear my brother yell my name, but I keep going.

When he hears my name, Que turns around, looks into my eyes and takes off running. The chase begins, but this time I'm not the prey. Terrell trails behind me as I focus on my target.

"Fuck boy, you tried to rob me!" I yell as I chase this scary nigga through the alley.

He hops over a rusted, short fence, and we jump it too. I almost lose my balance but Terrell is right behind Que.

"Keep up lil' bro," Terrell yells to me.

"No hard feelings, nigga," Que yells while looking over his shoulders at me.

His words only add more fuel to my fire. This nigga thinks this is a game. He takes me for a joke. I reach for the .45 caliber that's tucked in my pants—the one I stole two days ago from the pawn shop and the owner still is trying to find out who stole it.

"Kellz...no!" Terrell yells, but the gunshot blocks out his voice.

Damn, I missed him, so I fire the gun again and this time I got 'em. I fire again...and again until Que's body collapses to the ground. My brother shoves me and I lose my balance and fall onto the ground with the gun lying beside me.

"What the fuck you just do? He's dead!" Terrell screams as we both stare at the lifeless body in front of us. Streams of blood run down the concrete and all I can see is the aftermath of my revenge.

A few houses on the block begin to turn on their lights to be nosey. Hell, they should be used to this kind of activity around here. But I am pretty sure somebody is calling the cops.

"Oh, my God," Terrell mumbles, trying to fight back tears.

"Stop being a punk," I say, shocked by the weakness that my brother is showing. I know he didn't think I was gonna let his nigga try to kill me and then disrespect me again when we was chasing his ass. "Fuck that nigga, Terrell. We still got time to get away. Come on," I say to my brother, the only person in the world that I really gave a shit about.

He grabs me by my shirt and pushes me up against a brick wall.

"Our lives are over, Kellz! Can't you understand what you just did? We're going to spend the rest of our lives in jail for murder. Do you not get that?"

"I said we got time to get away."

"Look around," he says, making note of the people peeking out of their windows. A few of their nosey asses are even out standing on their porch, looking in our direction. "Somebody will snitch on us before we can make it home," he says.

"Well, at least you can get away. Go," I say, looking at Que's lifeless body and the growing puddle of blood around him. He deserved to lose his life, so I don't even know why we even discussing it. "Just leave me like everybody else, brah. I did it, I'll pay for it...fuck it," I tell Terrell. It's obvious he's spazzing over Que's bitch ass.

Terrell pauses for a second and we make eye contact. He's fighting back tears and I hate to see him like this. He's always been the one person I look up to.

"Nah, you're my lil' bro and I'll never leave you. You're all I got."

He releases my shirt and I say, "That's right, man. We got this, let's go."

"I love you more than life and I want you to know that. When I said I was your keeper, I meant that," Terrell says as he picks up the gun and starts rubbing his hands all over it.

"What are you doing?" I ask frantically.

He stares at me and tears begin to fall down his face. Seeing his tears makes my heart sink into my chest. The hell was Terrell doing?

"Kellz, you're young and have so much to live for. I never should've brought you here, so I'ma go down for this. Go home and tell grandma I love her and that I'm sorry—"

"No," I yell, cutting him off. I hug my brother and beg him not to do this. "Man, please don't do this brah. We can get away and it'll be their word against ours."

"Nah man, I'm taking the rap and that's my word, so go home like I said," he said with base in his voice. "And make something out of yourself. You only have one life...go live it."

My chest feels heavy and I start to sob like a lil' bitch. My brother is all I have. I need him to be here for me. I don't want him to be locked up behind a murder that I committed.

I push away from him, upset that he's choosing to give up. Terrell pulls me back and embraces me tightly.

"Go be somebody great, bro. You got the potential. You just have to leave these streets alone because it's nothing but trouble out here."

"Terrell, c'mon, man," I say looking around at our building audience.

He pushes me hard in the chest and says, "Listen to me, man, get the fuck out of here!"

I have never felt so bad in my life as I did then when I looked back at my brother's sad face.

"Just promise to hold me down," he says and I nod.

"I'm so sorry," I finally say.

It becomes quiet and I hear Terrell exhale. The tears just keep coming. I want to fuck something up because I'm 'bout to lose my best friend.

"Go on. Get out of here, kid. This will be our lil' secret," he says as sirens begin roaring in the distance. We embrace one last time.

"I love you."

"I love you too, lil' bro. Now go!"

I don't want to move, but Terrell pushes me to help make my feet move. Finally, I run behind a near dumpster and watch my brother for the last time as the ambulance picks up the body, and the police manhandle him to the ground to put him in handcuffs. I bet they are thinking he's just another sorry-ass thug that they got off the streets, but none of this was his fault.

I read the hurt and pain on my brother's face as he sits behind the police car. The scene tears me up inside and I cry all the way home. I don't want to leave him. And when my brother finally gets his day in court and the judge sentences him to life without parole, I begin hating everything and everyone. I will have to live this secret down for the rest of my life.

Chapter 1

KELLZ

Four Years Later

"Hood" is my middle name—Kellz "Hood" Smith. Everybody outside of the hood calls me Kellz. My dawgs from the hood call me K. Hood. When people look at me, all they see is a young thug with pants saggin', baggy shirt, and hat tipped to the side, but I'm really a nice guy. I just don't take crap from nobody. When I love, I love hard. But ain't no punk in me.

My demeanor attracts girls like a magnet, but so do my looks. I'll say I'm pretty decent looking. I'm around six feet three inches with caramel-colored skin and I got the body of my favorite rapper, The Game. Some even say I have the eyes of a killer.

Most niggas don't like me 'cause I'm the real deal. I get into frequent altercations at school or anywhere, because I'm the truth, and niggas always wanna test the truth.

Thuggin' is my lifestyle, and yeah, I walk the streets and sell dope, but there's something else that's important to me—well someone, I'd rather say. My girl Tamara is my life, my world, and my wifey. I love her fo'sho. We've been together since eighth grade.

There are only a few other things in my life that are important: my nigga Nick, my home girl Roxxi, and putting in this work and school. But I don't really care about school. I don't do nothin' there but get suspended. The only reason I go is because Tamara begs me to. I'd rather be on the corner slangin' dope and gettin' to the money. Like I said, I'm always in some type of trouble, which I frequently find a way to get out of.

I go back and forth between homes. It all depends on whose good side I'm on. Some nights, I'll just stay over my girl's crib. Her mom doesn't mind; she's barely home anyways.

My mom and I get along occasionally. The rest of my family can't stand to put up with me and my attitude. I say fuck 'em all. They ain't never done shit for me anyways! At the end of the day, I'm protecting the ones that matter, which is Tamara and her baby.

I know I got anger problems. I was assigned anger management classes, but I never go. It takes only a little to get me mad. I can't control it for some reason.

Life is rough for me, living on the edge. I take risks—even if it costs me my life.

Have I ever killed a person before? The answer is yes. Only one...long story short, I was thirteen, still in middle school, but my heart was in the streets. The streets was my teacher, and it taught me lessons I could never learn in a classroom.

Lessons like when that nigga played me over some dope money and tried to set me up with his boys. Just because I was thirteen, Que thought I wasn't up on game. When I caught on to his game, my brother, Terrell (who was nineteen at the time), went out to look for him. Next thing I knew, I was pulling the trigger, and the nigga was lying there lifeless. But Terrell had a plan; he took the blame for the murder, and he was sentenced life without parole. He didn't want to see me mess up my life at such a young age, but hell, as far as I could see, my life was already fucked up.

The judge described the homicide as brutal, horrid, and some other bullshit. All I could do was cry and, until this day, I still think about it. I try to visit Terrell every weekend, when I get the guts to do it.

He seems to always shed tears when I go, which makes me feel dead inside. I feel like it should be me inside those prison walls. I should be suffering the fate that he received for my crime. It's our secret until this day. While I'm out here walking these streets, I'll never forget it's Terrell behind bars. That's some fucked up shit.

When I turned fourteen, I got off two years' probation for selling drugs. I tried to change my life for the better. I wanted to walk the straight and narrow like I promised my brother I would do before he got locked up. But there's no good in me. I don't think I want to change.

I pull up in front of my homeboy C-Dog's house. I let out a sigh filled with grief. I'm so tired of thinking about all the shit I've endured in my short life.

"Sup K. Hood?" C-Dog says as I walk in and plop down on his couch.

"Damn, I'm tired folk!" I say angrily.

"Aye, making money ain't never easy," C-dog responds as my *I'm So Hood* ringtone begins to play. My phone vibrates like crazy in my pants pocket, but I smile because it's my girl Tamara.

"Yo' baby what's up?"

"Where the hell are you?" she yells in the phone. "You were supposed to call me back like three hours ago. You got me worried sick about you!"

"Chill, T," I say when I can finally get a word in. "I'm aiight."

"I'm serious, Kellz! Where the hell are you right now?"

Tamara has a nasty attitude, and I feel the tension building up in my chest. I don't feel like dealing with this bullshit at the moment.

"Whateva girl, you know I don't answer no questions like that."

"Oh, you gon' answer me, Kellz."

I can feel the tension rising up even higher in my chest. "Look! I ain't got time for this shit right now. You love gettin' on my damn bad side."

"What is that supposed to mean?" she says, sounding offended.

"It means you love pissin' me off."

"You don't ever have time for us anymore, and I'm the one pissing you off? Why don't you have time for us, Kellz? Is slanging drugs more important?"

"You know that's not true, T. I'm out here busting my ass for us. You know that."

"Prove it," she says pouting. "Stop doing what you doin', and come see me right now."

Damn! That's that shit she does to get on my nerves...always nagging about some shit...dumb shit, at that. I know after talking to her I'll need to smoke, so I motion for C-Dog to pass me the blunt he just rolled up. I take two long puffs out of it.

"Hello?" I finally say to see if she's still on the line.

"Did you hear anything I just said, Kellz?"

"Yeah, but listen, I'm going to finish this blunt. I'll call you back."

"You promise?" she sighs into the phone.

"Yes. I promise, boo."

With that being said, I hang up the phone, regretting that I yelled at her like that. I guess I fell asleep on the couch 'cause when I wake up, the house is quiet. I unlock my phone and begin flipping through the TV channels to find the game. There are three missed calls on my phone and two voicemails from Tamara.

Her first message informs me that she's stressing over Tremaine who was being fussy and cryin' about the way I talked to her. I turn the TV off and sit in silence for a moment. I sigh and take a moment to really think about my sexy girlfriend and how much she means to a nigga.

You're never supposed to mistreat the woman you love. I have plans to spend the rest of my life with this girl. I want to make her my wife. She was there through the good.

17

Supportive through the bad. She held a nigga down when a nigga didn't even deserve it. She has been my rock. She was there when I had nothing.

I guess I should make my way over there to comfort her. I love her, on everything. There's no better time than tonight to show her.

Chapter 2

TAMARA

Man life is crazy! Not only crazy, but complicated. I don't even know where to start. Let's see, I'm eighteen, barely passing the twelfth grade, and taking care of a baby that's not even mine. I am dating this guy named Kellz, and we've been going strong since middle school. I love this man with all my heart, and I can't imagine my life without him, but his ways are becoming tiresome. It's almost like babysitting another kid. I have to watch what I say to him because he can get mad in an instant.

Yeah...yeah, I know what you're thinking. Why didn't I leave him when I saw how he was in the first place? Well, that's because you can't help who you love. Yes he's bad for me, but he's good to me at the same time. He helps with the baby. He helps with food, clothes, and bills. You name it; he helps with it. I know the baby and I are his first priority, and there was a time when I never had to worry about him putting us last.

My mother is barely around. I pretty much take care of the house by myself. So you can add that stressor to my already complicated life. I have a fifteen-year-old sister who is grown as hell and don't care about anyone else but herself. She's always out at all times of the night, always staying in trouble at school, always fighting, always poppin' off at the mouth, and a whole bunch of other shit. I can't stand that little girl!

I see why my mother loves to stay gone, but at the same time I hate that she stays away. Most of these responsibilities I don't want. Sometimes, I just want to take myself away from it all, but then I remember Tremaine.

Tremaine is my one-year-old son, but really he's my sister's kid. She had him a year ago but never stayed around to take care of him. She doesn't know who his father is, so Kellz and I decided to take him in as our own. Well, not so much Kellz, although he helps, but a baby is the last thing on his mind right now. I've learned to accept that, although it bothers me a lot. I keep my mouth closed. I don't want to cause any trouble between us, so I'm just thankful that he helps.

I'm not really into my looks anymore. I guess I am okay. I'm not as gorgeous as my best friend Roxxi though. I stand about five feet six inches. I'm skinny at the top with wide hips and a lot of ass at the bottom. My hair is locked, and I've been growing my locks since the eighth grade, so it hangs a little past my shoulders.

I'm brown-skinned and, for some reason, everyone is in love with my eyelashes. I guess because they are so full, long, and curly. Because I don't work, it's kind of hard to keep myself up. Kellz may offer, but I don't take it. I feel as if he has done enough by helping with Tremaine.

I hope that I get it together soon. Graduation is around the corner, so I definitely need to buckle down when it comes to studying. It's just so hard to concentrate and focus.

I'm screaming for help, dying on the inside even, but I just hold it all in. I don't tell a soul—not even Kellz or Roxxi. No point in complaining to them. They can't help me.

I know I'm depressed, but I look for ways to tell myself that I am not. Sometimes I just want to die. I'm constantly screaming on the inside, "Lord take me now," but nothing happens. I just want it all to be fixed...and soon.

I look at Tremaine who is lying in my arms. Finally, he drifts off to sleep, and I exhale a sigh of relief. He has been so fussy over the past few weeks. This is actually the fussiest he has been in a while.

I place my son in my bed and smile. He's the only one that seems to calm my sea when my skies are storming. He depends on me, and I refuse to let him down.

I think of the other person who usually helps calm my sea, and my thoughts turn to Kellz. My heart sinks into my chest. There are days, such as this one, when he's barely any help with Tremaine. I wonder if this were actually his kid, would he be any different. He promised me we would be in this together.

Oh shut up, Tamara. Just be thankful for the shit that he does do. Don't be an ungrateful bitch. I look around at the pampers and outfits Kellz keeps us stocked up with. He gives what he can and sometimes more. Suddenly, I hear a car pull up in the driveway, pulling me from my thoughts. I look out the window to find that it's Kellz getting out of the car with a bag from McDonald's in his hand.

All of a sudden, my disappointment turns into happiness. I'm surprised I am so happy to see him pulling up. Or maybe I'm happy to see that he brought food. Or both. Either way, I rush down the stairs and swing the door open.

As he approaches the door, I wrap my arms around his neck, and we embrace in a tight hug. He squeezes, and suddenly I remember how much I miss his touch. "Hey, baby!" I say as a good feeling courses through every inch of my body.

"Sup, bae. I got you some McDonalds. I figured you were hungry."

I shrug as we walk into the house. "That's cool, babe. Thanks for thinking of me," I say as I follow him to the couch.

Kellz sits down onto the couch and places the bag on the end table. "No prob, shawty," he finally says. "You know I got you—even when we don't see eye to eye."

I smile and place a kiss on his cheek. "I love you," I tell him as I look into his eyes.

"I love you too."

"Do you want to know how much I missed you?" I say as I sit on his lap and start kissing him on his cheek before drifting to his neck.

"Damn girl. You really missed me, huh?"

I nod and continue to shower him with my kisses. He wraps his arms around my waist, and his hands inch up my shirt. Our lips meet with so much passion that I don't want it to end. My stomach growls in anger, and we both laugh.

"I think this can wait. You should eat," he says.

"You think so?" I ask, though getting up off his lap in agreement. Happily, I plunge into the bag to find all my favorites in it. Two apple pies, a chocolate chip cookie, a large fry, and a quarter pounder with no tomatoes or onions. "Awesome, babe. Thank you for getting what I like!"

As I take a huge bite out of my burger, my eyes turn to Kellz. He's staring off into space. It looks as if something is troubling him. I have never known Kellz to be the one to talk about his feelings. Normally, I would ask him what's bothering him, to which he always says nothing. I admire his strong willpower, but most of the time it's annoying. Sometimes, I feel as if he doesn't trust me with his feelings or his emotions. I can pour my heart and my soul out to this man, but he can't do the same for me. Why do I love him so much?

"What's wrong baby? Something bothering you?" I ask, hoping this time his reply will be different.

"Nawl. Why you ask?"

Just as I suspect, his feelings are closed off to me. "Well, it just look like you have something on your mind. I can read it on your face," I tell him.

"It's nothin'."

"You sure?"

"Yes...I'm sure!"

"Why are you yelling when you know Tremaine is sleep?" I ask. I can tell he is getting annoyed, but him getting annoyed for nothing is the type of shit that bothers me.

"'Cause I told you nothing was wrong with me, and you keep asking."

"I was—you know what, just forget it. I'm sorry."

"Sorry for what?"

"Sorry for getting on your nerves, baby." We were quiet for a minute, so I decided to change the subject. "Have you ate today?"

"Nope. Not hungry," he answers flatly.

"Sleepy? You seem a bit grouchy."

"No, I'm just tired, Tamara. I work too hard...but I got to."

"Yeah?" is all I say as I place the rest of my burger into the bag. I've lost my appetite.

I look at his tired eyes and the stress lines on his forehead. My man is right. He works so damn hard to get the things we need.

I grab Kellz's hand and motion him to lay his head on my lap. I rub his head softly and let out a wistful sigh. I just don't want to argue today. I don't want any animosity between us at the moment. If giving him a massage will do the trick, then I'm all for satisfying my man.

I kiss his lips, cupping his jawline and tracing my hands down to his strong chest. I slide my hand under his shirt and run my fingers through his chest hair.

"Can you stay for a little while longer?" I ask, my lips very close to his in intimacy.

He moans his answer as he sits up on the sofa and pulls me onto his lap. His hands roam over my body. "This is what a nigga needs after a day like this, Tamara," he says between sprinkling kisses over my chest and neck. His hand slips into my shorts and finds my heat.

I grab his hand and push it further into my panties as I moan.

"Damn, Mara, you so wet," he says with a deep groan. He unbuttons my shorts, and I stand up to remove them from my body. I take off my shirt, while Kellz is quickly coming out of his pants.

"Wet for you, Kellz. I missed you so much today," I say, ready to feel him inside of me.

He reaches in his pocket and gets a condom out and puts it on with haste. As soon as we're protected, he bends me over the sofa and makes us one. He wraps his arms around my waist and goes in deeper and deeper with each stroke.

I begin moving to match his strokes. Meeting his rhythm, I feel all woman.

"Mara, you got a nigga in love with this shit, man," he says as he speeds up like he's on a race to the finish line. He's hitting my spot so hard and fast that I can feel a hard nut coming.

"Kellz, I'm about to cum so fucking hard!"

He bends to the fold of my back and places his lips against the back of my neck, all while thrusting deeper and harder. "Cum for me, Mara," he says as his thrusts pick up speed.

Kellz growls each time my heat grips and releases him. I thrust my hips back onto him to heighten the intensity of his orgasm even more. He hollers my name as he jerks and bucks, filling the condom with hot semen. "Fuck! Mara! I love you so much girl."

The sound of him calling my name drives me over the edge. "Kellz," I cry out in the heated moment before my walls envelope his shaft and practically milk every drop of cum he has to offer, while my orgasm leaks from my heat in between vivacious pulsations. My hand cups both of my breasts to heighten the sensation. I crash down onto the sofa once he releases my waist. Kellz lies down beside me and brushes my hair to one side.

"I love that shit, baby," he says with his breath against my neck.

I feel so good in this moment that I have to encourage my man. "As long as we have each other, Kellz, we can get through it. God tells me so," I tell him.

Kellz is silent for a quick second. "Don't start with this God bullshit, Tamara. Not today..."

"It's not bullshit. It's the truth."

"Well, keep that truth to your got damn self."

As soon as he says that, I hush my mouth. His disrespect is something I don't deserve, but it's something I've been putting up with for all these years. You would think I'd be the one he respects. I was down for him when everyone else left him out in the cold.

As soon as that thought enters my mind, the same reasoning that keeps me under his hold enters my mind telling me to stop thinking about the bad things and to remember the good. He's never put his hands on me. His words are just words, and his actions speak otherwise. *You know he loves you...don't be an ungrateful bitch,* I tell myself as I recount the reasons why I love him so much.

"Bae, you know what?" he asks, finally speaking calmly.

"What's that, Kellz?"

He looks towards me. "I love you...more than anything in this whole world."

I really want to let a tear fall, but I hold it back. It'll only make the situation more awkward than it already is. Whenever he makes me doubt the way he feels about me, he always does or says something to brighten my world all over again. As much as I try, I don't think I'll ever understand his up and down moods.

"I love you too...more than anything in this world," I say, knowing I couldn't find it in my heart to let him go...or could I?

Chapter 3

NICKHOLAS

I slam my sweaty, tired body onto my bed and take a deep breath. I really brought my A game to the court today. That's only because we had some new niggas playing on the court. Otherwise, I wouldn't have tried so hard. I couldn't very well let them niggas come to our court and run up the score. My team won by five points, but it was a close game.

Luckily, I had a game changer move for them niggas. A move they didn't even see coming. I smile at myself as it replays in my head. Of course I was feeling myself, but that was beside the point. Everybody at the court knew my name, and those niggas was so full of themselves. I never broke a sweat, even when old dude was trying to get physical because he turned out to be a loser. They just don't know Nickholas doesn't fight. I'm way too handsome for that.

Pretty boy Nick is what I've been known as since grade school. Women are indeed in love with my looks. Standing over six feet; slightly built; light skin; long, curly, puffy hair with light brown eyes. I'm half Caucasian, half African-American and, to top it all off, they love my New York accent. New York is where I was born and raised most of my life.

29

When I turned fifteen, my parents decided to move to Georgia so we could settle as a family in a quieter, slower environment.

I have a pretty good life. Most say I'm spoiled, conceited, and arrogant. I don't go a day without hearing these three words. I have a love and passion for basketball. I can see myself playing in the NBA soon. I play at the court with some friends to improve on my skills. I want to be better than the best, the next Kevin Durant, LeBron James, Kobe Bryant. Shit, actually I want to be better

Basketball is my second priority, and school is my first. I've made good grades since grade school. My weakest subject is math though. I was and never will be any good with numbers, unless I'm fucking up some commas.

My third priority is Roxxi. I've had my eyes on her for a while. We've became closer friends since eighth grade, but I haven't made my move in like two years. I've been so distracted by other girls, which I know it makes her cringe, and I hate that. She's always accusing me of something or being with someone. Then it leads to her nagging, but that's my girl though.

My best friend is Kellz. We've been cool for a while too. And that alone is crazy because we're two different types of niggas. Our lifestyles are like oil and water, but we get along so well—except when he gets into one of his angry moods. Other than that, he's been a loyal-ass friend, and I'm going to be there for my dawg no matter what. I just try to stay on his good side. Therefore, no drama will be started between us.

Am I scared of my best friend? No...I'm just afraid of what he'll do.

I'm a pretty good dude. I stay out of trouble and don't have any enemies, unless girls are mad at me, but that doesn't last for long. I'm optimistic when it comes to life, and I smile even when it throws me lemons. It's nothing I can't handle.

I'm a sweet guy. I'm hardly angry or upset. I don't hold grudges. I keep my biggest goal in mind at all times: to be the next big NBA star.

I'm shaken out of my thoughts by my phone vibrating in my pocket. It's Roxxi calling—probably trying to see how the game turned out since she couldn't make it.

"Hello. What's up, Princess?"

"Hey my star player! How was the game? What are you doing? Did you guys win? Of course you guys did!" She talks so fast I can hardly get a word in.

Feeling a little awkward about the excitement in her voice, I clear my throat to get her attention. "Yo! The game was beast! I swear them niggas was mad as hell!"

She laughs. "Oh my—"

"What's up with all the questions anyway? You playing detective?"

She smacks her lips. "No. I'm just..."

She falls silent.

"Just what?"

"I'm just...excited to talk to you. That's all."

I smile. "Awl look atchu being all cute on me."

We both laugh, and it becomes quiet on the phone again. I hate moments like this. We like each other so much, 'til the point that sometimes we don't know what to say to each other. It's like we don't want to say the wrong thing or be corny or too flirty. We both are still in denial about us liking each other. I'm still getting comfortable with being open and sensitive with her. We've been friends for so long, so it's all new to me.

"Oh whatever," she finally speaks. "So, I heard that you and Veronica have a date planned next weekend. How come I'm just finding out about this?"

Damn. I should have known there was a catch to her calling me. She can never call to have a decent conversation without bringing other bitches into it.

"Uh," I murmur. "Yeah it's something like that, but not really."

"Boy, please. What do you call it then? You know you want her!"

I roll my eyes, ready to make this discussion as short as possible. "Whatever. I don't want her. I want you."

Roxxi giggles on the other end. "I doubt it."

I grunt at Roxxi's comment. "Okay. That's cool."

"You probably fucked her already."

My mouth drops open. Shorty is trippin' bad. Would it be any of her business if I had fucked Veronica? I contemplate whether or not I should tell her the truth, but hell she probably already knows with Veronica's big-ass mouth. "And if I did?" I ask her.

"Yeah, I already heard about it...and you weren't even going to tell me!"

"Yo, you be trippin'. Why the fuck are we even talking about her? It wasn't anything serious anyway."

"Lies," she yells. "I just hope you're not leading me on."

"Oh."

"Oh? Is that all you have to say?"

"I'll hit you back later."

"Why?"

"Because I got something to do."

"Oh, so now you got something to do?"

"Yeah."

"Whatever...you can't keep doing me like this, Nick."

"Bye, Roxxi," I say before disconnecting the call.

I didn't expect our conversation to go that way. But females stay trippin' over some bullshit. I don't know if I could ever be real with her. Her insecurity is her most annoying trait, besides her snorting when she laughs really hard. At least I find that kind of cute.

I gather my stuff for me to take a shower. I twist the hot water knob as far as it can go. A hot, relaxing shower is exactly what I need to calm my nerves. If anybody knows how to get under my skin, it's my bae, Roxxi.

Chapter 4

ROXXI

I remember back in middle school when kids used to annoy me with sayings like, "You can't play basketball: you're a girl! Why are you so manly?" These are the words I used to get taunted with. And literally, it freaked me out.

I remember running home to my mom crying. I believed what the other kids were saying was true. My mom would always tell me, "Oh they are just being kids, honey. You can be anything you want to be."

Of course, I took my mom's words as true—and still do 'til this day.

Roxxi is what everyone calls me. I stand about five feet seven inches with an athletic build. I am half African American and half Puerto Rican. I have smooth mocha skin and thick, long black hair that rests at the center of my back. Originally, I'm from Texas. My family moved to Georgia when my stepdad was offered a position at a growing company here. It's pretty much okay, but it is nothing like Texas.

I'm pretty good when it comes to my schooling. High school is so different from middle school—in a personal sense. In high school, I have people telling me how pretty I am and how well I can play basketball. *"Wow Roxxi! You should go pro...Your hair is so gorgeous...Gosh you're pretty!"* I get many compliments from guys but weird looks from most girls.

In middle school, I was always being picked on. I was chunky with a mild case of acne. A chunky Hispanic girl trying to play basketball. I wasn't into makeup, boys, or the latest fashion. Basketball was my only focus. As I got older, those things began to change, but I'll always have a love for basketball.

My best friend is Tamara. We have been friends since middle school, and to be honest, she's the only girl I trust. Of course, she had to earn that trust because, at first, she was one of the girls who use to pick on me. Later on in the school year, she saw I needed a friend. She apologized, and we just clicked from there.

We spent every day with each other. If we weren't talking on the phone, we were having sleepovers. If we weren't having sleepovers, we would hang at the mall. She taught me how to be confident in talking to boys and catching up with the latest trends. She's like my other half.

Speaking of my best friend Tamara, I admire her loyalty regarding her relationship with Kellz. Wow! They have been dating for four years. It's so inspiring. I hope one day Nick and I can accomplish the same thing. First, he needs to take control of his groupies. I know it's not a real relationship without trust, but I try so hard to tell myself that nothing is happening with those other bitches. Of course, he tells me this all the time, but I just know how these southern bitches are. They're grimy, conniving, desperate, and fake...like the thirsty thots I know them to be.

I love my family more than anything. Unfortunately, my mother is having another baby—a boy, and I'm not too happy about it. I mean, she has me and my brother. Why do we need another kid running around? My little bro is only three, and he's a handful by himself. So imagine our house with a newborn. It'll be noisier times ten, and that's the last thing I want, but my feelings don't matter.

I hardly say anything about the new baby, and when she talks about it, I brush it off and change the subject. I know it makes her feel some type of way, but not once did she ask me how I felt about the whole situation. I don't know whether to be happy, sad, or disappointed. I'm somewhere in the middle. I love to see her excited about having it, but...Ugh! I do not need another brother...damn!

On top of the addition to my family, I think about Nick and become annoyed with myself. Why do I care so much about what he does when we're not even in a relationship? I let out a big sigh as I silently question myself.

Me and my big mouth. All I wanted was for him to tell me the truth, but like always, he danced around it. Should I text him? Or call him back? I contemplate my next move for about twenty minutes then decide to text him a sad emoji face. Biting my lip, I wait impatiently for him to text back.

Damn, I got it bad. I love him so much. I just want us to be able to be real with each other. That's what couples are supposed to do.

Roxxi, get over yourself. You ain't even his girl—officially, I think just as a text comes through thirty minutes later. Finally, he texted me back apologizing for the way he reacted.

He confessed that he and Veronica fucked only twice but that it didn't mean anything to him. All of a sudden, my guilt over upsetting him evaporates. I knew in my heart that he'd been with Veronica. His texts slow down, and then he calls me and tells me how much I mean to him.

"My people are gonna be gone tonight. You wanna come over and chill?" he asks.

"Really?" I reply with a question, while trying not to sound too excited. On the inside, my stomach is doing flips. This is the moment I've been waiting for.

"Yeah really, ma. So you coming over?"

"Yeah, I guess I can squeeze you in."

He laughs. "Whatever. You know you want to keep daddy company. Better be lucky I asked you and not Veronica."

"Fuck you," I say, about to hang up on him.

He laughs again. "Just joking, baby. I can't wait to see you though."

I blush and sigh loudly into the phone. "Aw look atchu getting all cute on me," I remark.

"Yup, he says. "See you 'round nine?"

"Yea," I answer as my mind begins to race. Not race as in a bad hectic way but an "OMG, I'm going to spend time with bae" type of way.

I have to pick something cute to wear. Something sexy, but not too sexy. Something comfortable, but not too comfortable. I think I should show a lil' stomach and thighs. But maybe that's too revealing. A dress? No, too formal.

I decide to wear my crop top and high waist, acid wash jeans that curve to my body so well. I paint my fingernails and toenails, curl my hair, and decide to put on a little makeup. Just some eyeliner, eye shadow, and lipstick. I don't want to do too much. I mean, it's not like I'm desperate or anything.

I chuckle at my thoughts as I begin to play out the night in my head. Maybe some kisses here and some kisses there. Maybe some foreplay, but I definitely won't be giving up the cookies. Although, I've had many urges to do so when I spend alone time with him. I don't know why, but my gut always tell me to wait. Well, maybe I do know why. I mean, his smash list is like infinite.

Yes. Nick is a man whore. When he showed me the list, I almost gagged. He's had sex with over eighty women, and he's only seventeen. I'm surprised his penis hasn't fallen off from sticking it in so many different holes. But then again, that was the past. My man...my fine man...has turned over a new leaf, and he's all mine.

Chapter 5

KELLZ

I park in my mom's driveway and turn the car off. I lean back onto the seat and just sit there. I just left Tamara's house, and I'm too tired to do anything else. I just want to rest. My body, my mind, and my spirit are exhausted. I felt different as soon as I left my girl. I don't know. It's like my world gets darker when I'm not around her. My mood gets cloudy, and it's just so hard to tell what I'm going to be feeling next. But when I'm around her, I feel at peace; I feel happy, safe, and secure, even though I may not show it.

I close my eyes for a quick second until I hear banging on my car window. Of course, it's my mother bitching about something.

"Kellz, open this damn door!" she says with her constant frown lines resting on her forehead.

I roll my eyes and do as I'm told. "What is it, ma?"

"Boy, what did I tell you about bringing this shit in my house?" She holds up a bag of weed, and I wonder how she found it. I thought I had it well hidden. This only means this bitch was snooping in my room just looking for shit to bust me out on. "I told you, Kellz...Do not bring these drugs in my

41

house! If you want to smoke, then you need to take that shit over your homeboy's mama's crib, but not mines! I am so sick and tired of you, Kellz!"

She throws the bag of weed at me and places her hands on her hips. "Why can't you be the young man I raised you to be? Please don't turn out like your brother."

"Don't fuckin' talk about him! And I'm fine just like I am. If you were hoping for some dick-sucking goody boy, then I am not it. You need to go find his ass elsewhere. Why can't you love me for me, mama? Ask yourself that!" My chest begins to fill with rage, and my breathing becomes erratic.

My mama slaps me in the back of my head. "Boy, what did you say to me? I love you regardless but..."

"Fuck that! I'm leavin'. It ain't like living with you is the best damn place in the world to be!" I yell as I push her out my way and was about to head to my room to go get my things.

She uses all her strength to push me back into the car. She slaps me across my face this time, much harder than the first hit. I hold back the urge to slap her black ass back.

"Don't you ever raise your voice at me again, boy! I am still your mother, and you're going to respect me!"

"Then act like you love me," I yell. "Don't fuckin' judge me and then expect me to respect you. Don't go snoopin' in my got damn room then come at me on some fuck shit! You can just leave me the hell alone!"

She slaps me even harder this time, and I feel my face getting hot. "I will not leave you alone until you are grown and out of my house, Kellz. I can't believe you are my child! You don't have a legitimate job; you are in love with some girl who doesn't want to do shit with herself, and you're just a bad damn look! I didn't raise none of you this way."

"Aaaaaaaah! You can rot in hell!"

She raises her hand to slap me again, but this time I catch her and return the favor with the back of my hand. She screams like she has entered the gates of hell as she falls to the ground. Her sobs continue as I look down at my knuckles and see blood running down the sides of my hands.

I forgot I was wearing the ring she gave me when she thought she saw a change in me. That was during the time we were getting along so well. We laughed. We connected. We were in sync, instead of fighting like wild animals at a zoo.

I feel the hate in my heart towards my mother as I look into her sad eyes. She can't believe I struck her. What she doesn't know is I'm sad too. Sad that she can't love who I am. If she doesn't love me for who I am now, then she'll never be able to love me.

I twist the ring off my finger, and I throw it on the ground beside her. Leaving all of my belongings behind, I hop in my car and take off full speed.

Chapter 6

NICKHOLAS

A million and one things run through my head as I get off the phone with Kellz. He's in some type of trouble. The only thing he told me was he got into a fight with his mom. When I told him that's normal for them, he said this time it's serious. I send up a quick prayer hoping my boy wasn't stupid enough to put his hands on his mother.

I check the time. Kellz is on his way over, and Roxxi will be coming over in like an hour. Somehow, I have to get Kellz up and going before she gets here.

My phone rings, and it's my folks calling to let me know they're on their way to pick up my little brother, Devon, so I have to tell him to get ready. I walk into the kitchen to find him making a sandwich and still undressed. I glare at him. "Aye bro, why you ain't dressed? And Ma said to wear that ugly-ass button-up shirt tonight."

"Why I gotta wear that shirt?" he questions. "And I'll get ready in a minute. I'm hungry."

"Um, you are about to go to dinner. What's the point of the sandwich? You need to be getting dressed!"

He shrugs. "Why the hell you rushing me to get ready?"

"Who's rushing? I'm not rushing. It's just that black folks can never be on time for shit," I say, shaking my head. He laughs and bites a chunk out of his sandwich.

"True," he says with a mouth full of bologna.

Suddenly, the phone begins to ring. We both look at each other and then grab for it. I get to it first. "Hello?"

"Yo, who is this?" the female voice asks on the other end.

"Who this?" I mimic back.

"This is Daesha," she answers.

"Oh. Who you callin' for Daesha?" I look at my little bro, and his eyes get big when I say her name. He motions for me to tell her he's not home. I try hard not to laugh. I can't bust my lil' bro like that.

"I'm callin' for Devon. Is he home?" she asks.

"Nawl. He's not here ma, but I will gladly tell him that you called."

"Okay." She pauses. "Is this his brother?"

"Yeah."

She pauses again.

"Oh okay. Well, just tell him I called sexy," she says as I hang up the phone. I realize ol' girl tried to make a move on me.

"Nope, too young for you bro," Devon punches me in my arm and scowls at me. "Don't be tryin' to get with my girl!"

I laugh. "Dude please! She was flirtin' with me with her young, fast ass. You love them hot-in-the-pants chicks."

"Screw you," he says as he makes his way up the stairs.

The doorbell rings, and I open it to discover it's my boy Kellz.

"What's up, bro?"

We greet each other with brotherly dap.

"Sup."

"Yoooo Kellz! What's up, bro," Devon exclaims from the top of the stairs. "Where you been?"

"Shit...around. What you been up to lil' bro?" Kellz asks Devon.

"Being a playa," Devon responds nonchalantly.

Kellz laughs. "I hear you. How many girlfriend's you got now?"

"Hmmm, four and counting."

"Damn."

Devon rushes to his room as soon as he hears a car horn in the driveway. It's my parents. "Yoooo, what's up my peoples," I greet them as they approach the door.

"Fool, get out the way," my mother exclaims. "Hurry up Devon!"

As soon as my parents disappear upstairs, I motion for Kellz to give me the scoop.

"Nawl. I don't feel like talkin' about it at the moment."

The fuck. "Oh," I say slowly. "Well, how long do you plan on staying?"

Kellz looks at me. "Damn. You kickin' me out too, dawg?"

I chuckle. "Nawl. But I'm having company in the next thirty minutes."

"Company? Company with who?"

"A female."

"What female, nigga?" Kellz asks using his fingers to quote the word female.

"Roxxi," I finally admit.

"Damn for real?" he says with a laugh.

"Yea...What's so funny?"

"Nun," he answers as soon as he stops laughing.

I shoot him a confused look.

"It's nothin' brah," he says again. "Are you gonna finally hit it or seal the deal? You got to be doing at least one of those two things. You're the man if you do both."

"Hmmm....me having sex with Roxxi? My fantasy will finally come true when that happens. But for tonight it's neither," I answer truthfully. "Not ready for neither of those."

"Damn. It's been four years, motherfucka, and you still ain't ready? I mean, you already know how she feels soooo."

"I don't know. We may get to that point tonight."

"Which point?" Kellz asks.

"To the point of me officially asking her out."

"Yeah, whatever. I'll leave you two alone though."

"Good," I say, relieved that he was not pushing for more details about me and Roxxi. My peoples left for their dinner, and I went upstairs to take a shower and put on something comfortable.

"Nick! Your female is here," Kellz yells up the stairs.

I check in the mirror one more time and then make my way downstairs. Kellz is still sitting on the couch playing on his phone. But my girl Roxxi is looking right.

"Uhhhh Kellz..." I say, giving my homie a look that told him to get gone.

"Yeah, yeah, yeah...I know. I'm leaving now." He jumps off the couch, and we dap.

"See ya' man." I turn my attention to Roxxi. Her hips are hugging her jeans so tight, so right. We embrace in a hug. I lick my lips as if I can taste her sexy ass on my tongue. "Girl, those jeans though."

She laughs as she sits on the couch. "Shut up, fool. What are we watching tonight?"

I flash her a smile. "Whatever you want to watch. I wasn't planning on paying attention to the movie anyway."

"What were you plan on doing then?"

I don't say anything but instead grab her to sit her closer to me. I wrap my arms around her shoulders and place my hand on her thigh. The way she came over here looking in them jeans, I know she didn't just come over here to just watch a damn movie. I start to kiss on her neck and rub on her thigh.

"Ummmmm," she murmurs, enjoying every minute of our connection. Slowly, she pulls away from me.

"What?" I ask, wanting her back in my arms.

"I should be asking you that," she says with so many questions in her eyes.

I let out a sigh. "Go pick out a movie, babe. Your choice."

"Why you acting like that, Nick?"

"Like what?"

"Like you're getting annoyed with me."

"I'm not," I say, even though I really am annoyed as fuck that she keeps playing this game with me.

"What is it then? Why did your whole attitude towards me change in two seconds flat?" she asks.

"You're just always pulling away when I try to get closer to you. But you get mad when you hear about me touching other females. I don't get you. You're a big-ass contradiction."

"So you're mad with me 'cause I'm not trying to have sex with you tonight?" she asks.

I wave my hand and get up to put in the movie. That way we can watch a movie, and I can get her the fuck out my house.

"You mad or nah?" she asks again.

"Nah. Irritated...Very irritated. You can't bitch about shit that you don't even like doing with me, Roxxi," I say, and I'm over this damn movie night just that damn quick. I walk upstairs to my room, leaving her sitting there by herself. I know she's gonna come upstairs after me. Just had to give her time. That's how the game is played with Roxxi.

Chapter 7

ROXXI

No this nigga didn't leave me down here by myself. The fuck got into him. Should I go home? Or should I go upstairs to talk to him? I just don't understand how he became irritated. I know what he's tryna do, and I'm not ready to go down that road with him yet. I know when a guy starts kissing on your neck and feeling on your thigh, he's leading to one thing. It just has me wondering if he sees me the same way he see's other women. I thought I was special to him. I thought I was different.

Why would he try to go there with me?

Finally, I decide to go talk to him. When I get to his room, he's lying on his bed staring at the ceiling. He smiles when I sit beside him on the bed.

"Bout time you showed up, Roxxi. What's up?"

"It's not that I am trying to pull away from you. I just thought you looked at me different from those other girls. I thought we had a connection that has to do with more than just sex." Nick gives me a puzzled look, and all of a sudden I'm embarrassed for expressing my feelings to him. "Never mind," I say and look away from him.

"Sex? We do have a connection that's more than sex." He laughs. "Oh! Is that what you thought I was trying to do downstairs?"

I nod and feel stupid because he's laughing. "It's not funny, Nick."

"Yes it is, babe. Look," he says as his laughing subsides, "I'm sorry if I came off too strong. Girl you know your kitty is gold. I'm not trying to take it there until you're ready. You already know how I feel about you. There's no need to think differently of me." He grabs my hand and kisses it.

Suddenly, I feel relieved. I was so silly to even think that.

"Well, if that's the case, why can't we be more than just friends?" I ask, stopping abruptly as I register what I've just said. I'm shocked those words even came out my mouth; if only I could take them back. I feel embarrassed again. This time, I know my face is turning red. I just feel weird showing this side to him.

I look at him, and his expression is warm. He smiles and says, "I was waiting on you, Roxxi."

I feel happy with the feeling of butterflies in my stomach. "Really, Nick?"

"Yeah. Whenever you are ready."

"I am ready. But..."

"But what?"

His answer to this very simple question would show me whether he meant business or not. "Will there be any more women or just me?"

"Of course, it'll be you and you only—my one and only. I wouldn't have it any other way, babe. Come here." He motions for me to lie on his chest, and it feels so good to feel his touch as he wraps his arms around me. He kisses me on my forehead. I know this is too good to be true. It has to be. "I got you babe," he says.

My stomach begins to do backflips, and my heart begins to flutter. For once, I feel like I've died and gone to heaven. A dreamy, silly smile attaches itself to my lips and blooms full force. "So what does this mean?" I ask.

Our eyes meet, and we begin to kiss.

"You're my girl," he says as we pull apart. "Officially," he adds, and the butterflies in my stomach begin anew as he looks at me in the way he does.

We lie there in each other's arms for an hour before making our way back downstairs to watch a movie. We make out about halfway through the movie, then it's time for me to leave. My body doesn't want to go, but my feet drag towards the door.

I can finally sleep tonight knowing that he is mine...all mine.

Can I really believe that Nick will be faithful?

Of course you can, Rox, I tell myself as I walk out of his door with his sweet kisses lingering on my lips. Trust is a major part of a relationship, and if I don't trust him, we might as well call it off now. But there is no way I'll call it off, not after waiting four years for this shit to happen. I tell myself that we're going to be okay because I believe in my heart that everything will work out just fine.

Chapter 8

KELLZ

I'm dreading the rest of this school day. I place all my books in my locker, and all of a sudden, I feel a tap on my shoulder. I turn around to find Kimmy smilin' in my face. Kimmy's the chick who has been feelin' me since the beginning of my senior year. We ain't never do nothin'. For one, she isn't appealing, and for two, I got Tamara.

Kimmy told me she had a thing for bad boys. But whatever bullshit fantasy that's going through her mind is dead as fuck.

"Sup," I say, shrugging her off.

"Hey, Kellz. What trouble you gettin' into today?"

"I don't know. The school day just started." I close my locker and turn around to find her all in my face with her mouth to my forehead. She looks up at me.

"I missed you this weekend. How come we never link up?"

"For one, you ain't my girl. And for two, its word your kitty running loose. Save that shit for them hoe-ass niggas you mess with." I shove her to the side and walk off towards Tamara's locker. Some tall, lanky nigga is standing at

Tamara's locker talkin' her, and I instantly feel disrespected when they both begin to laugh.

"Aye, what you doin' with my girl, dawg?" I step in between them, and dude freezes in his place. "I'm talkin' to you, nigga!"

Tamara tugs on my arm. She kisses me on my cheek and smiles. "Babe, We ain't doin' nothing but talking."

"Oh, who is he?"

Tamara rolls her eyes. "Do you have to be so rude, Kellz?"

"Who are you, brah?" I ask, flexing my chest at this nigga who unknowingly is about to get his shit split. Nobody, and I mean nobody, stands around in this hallway flirting with my girl.

"Um. Chauncey...Chauncey Snipes."

He pulls out his hand for me to shake it. I glance at him like he's crazy. Slowly, he pulls it back.

"What the hell you got to talk about with my girl?" I ask.

"Excuse me, Chauncey," Tamara says as she pulls me to the side. "What do you think you are doin'?"

"Nothin'. Just askin' a nigga some questions."

"Yeah, but that's not how you talk to people."

"Yeah, whateva. You about to get people dealt with. Why you in this hall flirting and smiling and shit."

"Since you want to know, Chauncey is my study partner for chemistry. He's getting good grades, and I really have to get my shit together with school so I can graduate."

"Oh," is all I say.

"Yeah, oh," she says with attitude. She walks past me back to her locker, where Chauncey's punk ass is still standing. "Sorry about that, Chauncey," she apologizes for my behavior.

Did she really just diss me for this nigga? I try to be reasonable, but this shit isn't sitting well with a nigga who's supposed to be her man. I know she trippin' because this shit ain't gon' happen today. I snatch her by her arm and pull her back to me. "What is your problem, Tamara? I know you're not disrespecting me for this fuck nigga."

She looks at me like I'm all crazy or sumthin'.

"I don't have a problem, Kellz. Now let go of me!"

"Don't you ever do no shit like that again!" I tell her while squeezing her arm tight. I can feel my anger rising so high. I want Tamara to understand that I don't play this shit.

"You're hurting me!" she says as she struggles to get out of my hold on her. By then, I had caused a scene in the hallway. Everybody stops and stares at us.

"The fuck yawl lookin' at!" I yell at the building crowd.

Suddenly, this Chauncey nigga grabs my arm and snatches it away from Tamara. I step into his face and shove him. "What you think you doin', lil' nigga?"

He pauses. "Tamara, is this really what you consider a boyfriend? You deserve better than this clown," he says before stomping off with a heated look on his face. "I'll see you in class," he tosses over his shoulder.

His words stung like the slaps my mama gave me the other night. As soon as he walks away, I try to grab for his lil' ass, but somebody grabs my arm. It's Nick.

Tamara slams her locker and looks at me. She's furious and fiyah is in her eyes. She huffs at me then storms away in the same direction Chauncey went.

"Yo' what were you thinking?" Nick asks.

I shake my head. "Fuck him."

"You was ready to whoop his ass."

I smirk. "Shut up."

"Look, Kellz, you can't be getting into trouble this semester fam."

"What's so different about this semester? Shit, they all the same to me."

"This time, you're going to get expelled, and graduation is only three months away."

"Who gives a fuck," I reply. "School ain't makin' me no money. Just holdin' a nigga back. Nobody is keepin' me locked down."

"No, an education is what you need to survive out in this world. You can't sell dope forever. And I give a fuck. You're my nigga, and I'm just looking out for you."

I turn to look Nick in his face. I really don't give a damn about the shit he's talking about at the moment. I can't wait to get out of this prison anyways.

"Yeah, thanks for your lil' pep talk homie, but I'm kinda pissed right now. So if you could back off, I'll be on my way to class to get this all-American education so I can get my part of the American dream," I say sarcastically. With that being said, I walk away just not giving a fuck.

Chapter 9

TAMARA

I don't even know what just happened back there. It went from zero to a hundred real quick. I should've expected that from Kellz though. He's such the jealous type. I know he's going through a rough time right now, but I just can't have him scaring off my study partner that I'll have for these next three months.

Graduation is around the corner, and chemistry is the only thing holding me back from walking across that stage. I'm failing miserably, so I need exceptional grades in order to pass. Chauncey is my only ticket out. This high school diploma may not be important to Kellz, but it is to me.

I love him to death, but it's time for him to control his anger or...or...I'm gone! I stare at my chemistry test. I can't remember a damn thing I studied last night. It's so hard to study with Tremaine being fussy all night and unable to go back to sleep. I sigh and place my head on my desk. Fuck my life! My miserable, shitty-ass life!

The guy behind me taps me on my shoulder and hands me a folded piece of paper. He nods his head towards the back where Chauncey flashes me a smile and gives me a wink.

I turn around and impatiently unfold the paper. It has all the answers on it plus a side note at the end: *We can meet at the library this Wednesday after school and study this stuff then, beautiful.*

I feel relieved as I give him a thumbs up and begin to fill in the answers to my test. When class is over, I run to thank Chauncey with a hug.

"Thank you! I appreciate what you did so much," I say as I hug him.

He embraces me back. "No problem, beautiful. Our only focus is graduating, right?"

I nod as I stare at him. He's cute but a slick cute though. He stands at an average height, he's slim with a caramel skin tone. He resembles the rapper T.I. in a way.

"You know," I start off, "you kinda sorta look like—"

"T.I.," he finishes my sentence. "Yeah, I get that a lot."

"Really?"

"Yup. Except I don't rap, nor do I have that kind of money," he laughs.

"Well, what do you do?" I ask being curious.

"I dance, cook, write, and draw..."

"Oh really? And what kind of dancing do you do?"

"Street dance."

"Like Chris Brown?"

He laughs again. "Yeah, like Chris Brown."

"Cool. I guess I'll have to see you dance one day."

"Of course...my studio is always open. And by studio I mean the patio in my backyard."

I laugh.

"Awl man...you're funny," I say as I smile at him. He returns the gesture.

It becomes quiet between us, but I notice that our vibes are in tune with each other. I almost feel comfortable. He feels familiar to me, as if I have known him for a while. But of course, he's just the nerdy guy in my chemistry class.

Before we got paired up as study partners, I had passed by him a few times, and we spoke to each other every once in a while. He would try to spark up a conversation, but I was never interested. He sat by himself most of the time and didn't really make conversation with a lot of people. That was until half the class was failing, and we found out he was exceptionally gifted in chemistry. Then we were all begging for his help.

I wasn't one of them, but I gave him a few hints here and there. Finally, I got up the nerve and wrote him on Facebook asking for his help—only if he could. He agreed. And he promised that I would be passing this class with a B or higher. That's all I needed to hear.

"So what's up with you and the guy from hell? Do you really like this guy?" He puts emphasis on the word *really*. The look on his face says, *you can do so much better than a street thug.*

"What? You don't like him?" I respond sarcastically.

He chuckles and shakes his head. "Hell no. I've heard a lot about that guy. I'll just tell you now, he's not the one for you. Honestly, I don't think you deserve to be with that fool." He pauses, then continues, "I mean, he's into gangs, drugs, saggy pants...and apparently yelling at females. Soon, he's going to start beating on you...the way he put his hands on you earlier..." He leaves his comment unfinished, but I see the look of disgust on his face.

"What are you talking about, Chauncey?" I question. I can feel my temples begin to flare as I glare at him.

"Don't shoot the messenger, Tamara. I've met and conversed with a lot of guys like him. Those type of guys are messed up in the head. They're never in a position to care for a woman, let alone love her or show her some respect. The guys I've known, they were abusing their women, stealing from their women, and violating their women. I mean, it's crazy. A good girl should never fall in love with a thug."

As I take in all the information he's spilling to me, I want to call it bullshit. I mean, after all these years, Kellz has never put his hands on me. But then, I think about him hitting his mama. People always say if you want to know how a man will treat you, watch how he treats his mama.

Well, in this case, the bitch probably asked for it, I reasoned with myself. I've been there for him more than she has. She has turned her back on him time and time again. A mother's love should be unconditional. I love him even when he's at his worst...that in itself says a lot about my commitment to my man.

"I'm sorry Chauncey, but Kellz isn't like that," I assure him. "We've been together for four years, and he has never hit me."

"Just give him time. He definitely has a tendency to be violent. I can't believe you don't see it. Don't let the love you feel for him blind you to the facts that are staring you straight in your beautiful face, Tamara. If I could give you any piece of advice, it would be to leave him while you can...before it's too late," Chauncey says with so much concern in his eyes.

I study him, taking in his sincerity, and I almost go there with him for a second. Almost. But then, I wonder who does he think he is to tell me about Kellz, my boo of four years. Standing here spittin' all this so-called knowledge off at the lip. Nah, this fool is talking crazy. I could never leave my baby. He means everything to me. I know, I don't deserve the disrespect from Kellz, but I can't live without him.

What about finding your happiness? Are you truly happy? I ask myself, warring between whether or not my relationship is bullshit or pure bliss.

"Sooooo, we're definitely on for Wednesday, right beautiful?"

"Yeah," I say with a nod. I feel deflated.

"Great! So I'll catch you around, beautiful!"

He gently slaps me on my arm and goes on his merry way.

I notice how often he calls me beautiful. Kellz hasn't told me that since we started dating four years ago. He hardly tells me how beautiful I look—even when I splash on a tiny bit of makeup. He never notices the difference. I don't believe I'm beautiful. I can't be. All I have is ass and hips. It attracts men, but the wrong type of men. None of them tell me how beautiful I am. All I hear is "Damn girl, you're thicker than a snicker!" Or "Got damn! That ass though, or you're bootylicious!"

I can go on and on with so many derogatory statements from men. But Chauncey...he called me beautiful. Did he really mean it or was it just something to say? And if Kellz was going to hit me, wouldn't he have done it by now?

The jabbering thoughts continue in my head for the rest of the day, while Kellz blows up my cell phone. I don't really feel like talking because so much is running through my mind. I'm frustrated and irritated with Kellz right now, and it's all because Chauncey called me beautiful.

I wonder if he will call me beautiful again and if he means it. We seem like two different types of people, but I know we can learn from one another. He has a whole different type of lifestyle, but I think we click so well. Will he accept my background? My kid? My past? So many questions run through my mind about the possibility of being with Chauncey.

Girl, please. He doesn't want you. He likes those intelligent-type girls who get accepted into Harvard. And you? You haven't even applied to any colleges yet. Hell, you're barely passing any of your classes. You ain't shit. I sigh, almost wanting to cry as my reality sinks in.

I head to the kitchen when I hear my stomach growl. I got off the bus a few hours ago and haven't ate yet. Hell, it prolly ain't shit in the fridge no way. I open the door and look in, and just like I thought...nothing.

"When are you going to go grocery shopping, ma?" I ask my mother who is sitting on the sofa smoking a cigarette.

My mom places her hand on her hip and gives me that stank look that lets me know she's about to say some dumb, off-the-wall shit. Why did I even bother to ask her that damn question?

"We'll go grocery shopping when you get a damn job! Get off your ass Tamara and go to work!" I grunt aloud at her reply. "I don't care about your damn attitude. If you spend as much time looking for a job as you do with Kellz, then the fridge could be stocked with food. I can eat at my boyfriend's house. What about you? Oh yeah, your nigga livin' on the streets! Both of yawl some bums!"

"Fuck you," I yell. "Bitch!"

"Whatever," she says as she rolls her eyes. She begins to laugh obnoxiously as she grabs her Coach purse to head out the door. "I'm going to Kwan's house...to eat. Don't wait up!"

Just then, a tear falls down my face. I'm so heated and upset that I have forgotten how hungry I am. I just want to punch the wall. I fear for the life of my child, as well as my own. I can't allow him to see his mother struggle like this. I can't allow my baby to starve. Suddenly, my sister walks in with a guy behind her.

"Who is he?" I ask.

"Don't worry about him. He's with me. Geez, are you crying again? Why are you so damn emotional?" she asks as she grabs ole dude's hand and leads him to her room, or should I say her service room.

I have no doubt that my sister is fuckin' for money. How else would she be able to afford her Brazilian hair or acrylic nails? And of course, it's always some nigga cakin' her ass. She may be fifteen, but she don't look it. My sister is blessed with the hips and ass that our mama gave us, but she has the body of a stripper. She's thick as hell and a lil' lighter than me, and men just fall for her. Is she pretty? Prettier than me, in my opinion.

I try to set my mind on the TV as I surf the channels, until there's a knock at my door. A loud and harsh knock. Whoever it is seems angry.

I open the door and Kellz is standing before me. I should've been surprised, but I'm not. I've been ignoring him, so I knew he would show up here.

"I know you seen me callin' yo' ass," he says as he barges through the door. "You frontin' on me? Huh?" I roll my eyes and he yells, "Answer me!"

"Calm down, Kellz!"

"Calm down? I pay yo' fuckin' phone bill, so when I call you, you should answer. Don't front on me, T! What? You fuckin' wit that nigga that was at yo' locker? Huh?"

"No!" I vehemently deny.

"What's up then, T? Huh?"

He starts to close in on me, and suddenly I feel fearful to be in his presence for the first time. The flames in his eyes dance of the devil, and all I can see is red...A pitch fork in his hand would complete the diabolical picture. He grabs my wrist with full force and slightly turns it.

"Ow, you're hurting me, Kellz," I scream from the intense pain wrenching through my wrist.

"Don't front on me fo' some otha nigga, Tamara! I gave you four years of loyalty and honesty! Don't fuck me over!"

He throws my arm out of his reach, which causes me to almost stumble over. My whole body is shaking uncontrollably. I've never seen him so mad at me. Hot tears flow down my face like a river, and I shrivel in fear on the side of the couch.

It feels so unreal! My wrist is turning red as it aches and throbs with pain. So much hatred and disappointment floods my heart in that moment. I let out a crying shriek as I hear the door slam behind Kellz. My sunshine is turning into stormy clouds.

I hear Tremaine crying, but I have no strength to get up and go see about him. All I can do is cry along with him and cradle my swelling wrist from the wincing pain.

Chapter 10

ROXXI

"Come here Jayden!" My little brother Jayden walks towards me, and I lift him in my arms to plant a kiss on his cheek.

"Roxanna, I have to work late tonight, so I need you to watch your brother for me," says my mom as she pulls her hair up into a bun.

"Why can't Jessie do it?" I ask.

"Because, honey, he is exhausted from work. Plus, he has loads of paperwork to finish," she says. I glance down towards my mom's belly. She is in her seventh month.

I still don't understand why she chooses to work. Hell, Jessie moved us down here and knocked her ass up. Why can't he take over all the bills?

I don't dare speak my words aloud for mom to hear. "Great, I'm stuck babysittin' again," I say.

Now don't get me wrong, I love my little brother, but I do have a life. I'm stuck babysitting him as if he's my own kid, unless he is in daycare during the day, while I'm still in school. I'm just saying, if both of them are too busy for one kid, how in the hell are they going to have time for another one?

"Plans tonight?" she questions while giving me a concerned look.

"Maybe. It sure wasn't babysitting."

Jayden motions for me to put him down. "Night, night," he says as he tugs on my pajama pants. Before he heads to bed, my mom places a kiss on his cheek, and he waddles to his room.

"Okay, give me a sec, and I'll be in there to tuck you in, Jayden," I say. My mother is too busy getting ready for work to do it, and Jessie is too caught up in his 'paperwork.'

"Whatever Rox. I'm not in the mood for an argument tonight. I just don't understand you lately." She pauses before going on with her ranting. "Your attitude sucks, and you've been distant. I know you are worried about the new baby and all—"

"No, I'm not," I intervene with a frown on my face.

I begin to run the water in the sink so I can do the dishes. Sometimes, I feel like a damn maid in this house. I slam the dishes into the sink.

"Well, it's too late to have an abortion, Roxanna! There is nothing I can do!"

"Something you should have done was to keep your legs closed. Have you ever heard of using protection?" Those harsh words have been building for a while and fly out my mouth even before I can stop them.

Whap!

The sound resounds loudly in the kitchen as Mom lays a smack on my face without any hesitation. She tugs on my arm with strength I didn't even know she had, and her fingers bite into my arm.

"Ouch!" I try to tug my arm away from her painful grip. Mom's strength is too much in her anger.

"Now you listen to me, and you listen to me good. Don't you ever fix your mouth to speak to me in that way again. I'm having this baby whether you like it or not!"

Tears begin to fall down my face as I feel my heartbeat becoming stronger with every breath. For one, my mother has never hit me. For two, I have never spoken so low and sassy to her.

We were like best friends before she announced her pregnancy. Since then, shit has been rocky between us, and maybe it's all my fault. But I can't help the way I feel. She grabs my chin. "Do you hear me, lil' girl?" asks Mom.

I snatch her hand away from my chin and take off to my room. Fuck that and fuck her—and the baby. I feel my body shaking, so I lie down on the bed so I can catch my breath. Hot tears streak down my cheeks. I angrily dash them away. The moment between Mom and I was so intense; my heartbeat still isn't under control.

I pick up my phone to dial Tamara's number so I can let out some of my emotions to someone I can fully trust. I hope venting to her will release some of my steam.

"Girl, you will fall in love with the new baby," she reassures me. "Plus, you and Nick about to pop one out soon." She begins to laugh as if her remark is funny. I don't find anything comical about her pun. "Girl, cheer up! You're

71

about to go away for college...You will barely see the new baby anyway, so just chill," she tries to get me to see reason.

"Yeah," I say as my voice trails off. I never thought about that. The college I've been accepted into is just an hour and a half outside of Atlanta, which is about an hour and thirty minutes away.

"But giiirrrlll, I have something to spit to you," Tamara says sounding excited.

Beats talking about my problems, I think. "Aiight. Spill it."

"So as you know, Kellz acted a fool this morning by my locker when he saw me talking with this guy named Chauncey. He caused a scene and everything."

"Nothing new," I reply frankly.

"True, but anyways...Chauncey is a guy in my class who is tutoring me for my Chemistry class...in case you were wondering who he is. But girl, he's so charming. Like he called me beautiful after every sentence he spoke, and Rox, I barely hear that from Kellz. Like it kinda felt amazing, you know? Like wow...I'm beautiful."

"Of course you are, T."

"Nawl, you're my best friend. You're supposed to say that. But a guy noticed my so-called beauty before he noticed my booty, and that was amazing. Ya' know?"

I fall silent as I try to find the words to say to her. Of course, I'm happy that my girl feels this way. I don't want her to get in way over her head though. "That is amazing, T," I finally say. "And you deserve someone to tell you that."

"What you mean?"

"I mean, you are beautiful and deserve to hear it every day."

"Oh," she replies. "But guess what else he told me?"

"What?"

"He said that Kellz may start beating on me."

I start laughing at her nonsense. Now, she was talking ludicrous. "Girl you crazy! Kellz will never hurt you. He loves you too much. Besides, wouldn't he have done it by now if he was going to be abusive?"

"Same thing I said. But...I don't know. His anger is becoming too much to bear. It's so hard for us to communicate now," her voice trails off, and I can tell she has more to say but probably doesn't know how.

"So, what are you saying, T?" I ask.

"I don't know...just tired Rox. I don't know what to think right now. I just need to clear my head, so I'll see you tomorrow girl. Bye."

Before I can speak, she hangs up, and I hear the dial tone. Call me crazy, but it sounded as if Tamara was digging this new guy and hesitant about letting Kellz go. If she does let him go, that is four years down the drain.

My mind reflects back on Nick and him talking to those girls. Deep down, I'm not so sure I can trust him, but I want to so bad.

Roxxi, don't go thinking all crazy and psych yourself out. You're good. He's good. Nothing to worry about. I hope.

Chapter 11

KELLZ

I inhale and blow out smoke from the blunt I'm smoking then pass it to my homeboy. A lot is runnin' through a nigga's head, and smokin' is the only thing that relaxes me. My heart is heavy. I keep picturing the hurt on Tamara's face when I grabbed her. She seemed so frightened.

Man, I don't want to lose her, especially over no Bel-Air lookin' nigga. He isn't her type. He ain't gon do for her how I do for her ass. I gave her four years of my life. I could've cheated and fucked some random hoes. Trust me, I had plenty of opportunities, but the one person I don't want to hurt is Tamara. Temptation isn't shit to me.

"Aye, here you go K. Hood," my homeboy Terrance says as he passes me the blunt. I take three good puffs from it, and my thoughts keep rambling in my head. "You straight?" he asks, noticing my mood.

I nod. "Fa sho. Just having girl problems mane."

My homeboy Shad smacks his teeth. "You and Tamara? No way."

"Yeah. She fuckin' wit some gay-lookin' ass nigga. Just hope she ain't frontin' on me."

"You know shawty ain't leavin' you. You've been too good to her," Terrance proclaims. "And if she does leave you, then she wasn't shit from the start."

"Watch your mouth, dawg!" I warn him. I don't give two fucks about what me and Tamara going through, ain't nobody bout to sit in my face and disrespect her.

Terrance shrugs. "I'm just saying. Bitches ain't shit."

I sit up in my seat and glance at my nigga to let him know I want him to shut his damn mouth before I cause some problems. Then, out of nowhere, an all-black Ram truck rides past Terrance's crib slowly. The tinted windows make it so we can't see anyone inside.

"Who dat?" Shad asks.

I automatically reach for my pistol; Terrance reaches for his weapon as well. "I don't know, but some shit bout to go down," I reply.

We don't play that shit in the hood. If a nigga roll by slow, lights on or off, we automatically think it's either some niggas tryna rob or some niggas tryna open fire.

"Yo, we haven't seen Cash em in days. You think it's em niggas tryna rob us folk?" Shad asks.

"Nah," Terrance says while puffing on the roach.

"Cash locked up. And you know his niggas ain't gon' bust a move without his ass. Pussy-ass niggas." Terrance passes me the roach, and I finish it off.

Five minutes later, we see the truck again. This time, it stops in front of the house. I'm too high for this dumb shit. I grip my gun, and we wait for whoever's inside to show their face. A short, heavy-weight, bald-headed nigga steps out the truck holding a cane.

He's dressed too sharp to be anywhere from my hood. As he slowly makes his way up the sidewalk, I stand up and point my gun at his dome.

"Yo. Who are you and what you want?" I question him bluntly.

The man holds up his hands as if he is surrendering to the cops, and then he chuckles. "Don't shoot me kid. I'm good peoples. Put the gun down."

"Not until you tell me who the fuck you is and why you here?"

"Jimmy aka J-Money Bands and I'm here because I am lookin' for this brother who goes by the name K. Hood."

"Why?" Shad chimes in. "What you want wit 'em?"

"To talk business," J-Money says placing his hands down.

"Cash business?" I say, while slowly halting my gun and tucking it back in my pants. "How much cash you talkin', J-Money?"

"I want to speak with you alone," he indicates. He motions for me to step towards his truck.

As I follow him to his truck, I turn around and signal my niggas to watch my back, just in case shit got real.

"I heard about you," he starts off. "You are a money maker, and I like that."

I'm puzzled but feel good about his compliment. I really want him to get to his point.

"Your point, J-Money?"

"You can really bring in the money, and I mean lots of it. I heard you're a hard worker, and I need a nigga like you on my team."

I'm becoming impatient listening to his senseless yacking.

"What team? Get to the point."

"No family," he continues. "Gotta girl you really care about. She has a baby. No home. No car..."

"The fuck! Nigga, have you been keepin' tabs on me and shit?"

"I've been watching you for a while. Just around here. I'm tellin' you son; I can change your life around to where you and your girl ain't gotta want for shit. You can bring bands after bands by the day. Just hop on my team."

The shit he was spittin sounded good, but I couldn't trust this motherfucka as far as I could throw 'em. Bands, I can tell by the way he was ridin' he had to be pullin' in some type of cash.

"Nice truck," I say with a nod.

He looks at the truck and back at me. "Just bought it, straight cash last week...rides good. He can be yours, if you want him. Or you can make the bands to buy one yourself."

"Don't fuck with me, J-Money."

"No fuckery intended."

"How come I've never heard about you?"

"I'm top notch, but I stay low key. But hey, if you're interested in what I'm offering K. Hood, come by the strip club on 17th street tomorrow night around ten. Tell my peoples I sent you." He gets into his truck and cranks it up.

He rolls down his window to say, "I hope to see you there mane." With that being said, he speeds off.

I don't know if this is opportunity knocking or a setup. I want to talk to Tamara to see what she thinks, but her phone keeps ringing. After I fuckin' told her about answering the damn phone, she still isn't answering. I'll show her ass at school tomorrow though.

Chapter 12

TAMARA

"I'm not feeling today, at all," Roxxi groans. "The fight with my mom keeps replaying in my head. This morning, we didn't say anything to each other, which put Jessie in an awkward place. He attempted to spark conversation, but neither one of us was having it," Roxxi sighs heavily as she throws her books in her locker. "Fuck it, T. I'm just ready to move out of there."

I turn to her, ready to console her when Nick sneaks up behind her and places his hands over her. He motions for me to be quiet. I smile at the sweet way he plays with her. I wish Kellz would play little games with me like that, instead of rolling up on me with accusations and bullshit all the time.

"Guess who?" Nick says, and Roxxi turns around to embrace him in a hug and a kiss on the lips.

Nick is wearing skinny, black dress pants with some Stacey Adams topped with a white button-up and black tie, and his hair is gelled and neatly put into a pony tail. "Oh look at you! My handsome man. You look rather charming today.

"Thanks, babe."

"What's the occasion?" Roxxi asks.

"Gotta business presentation this morning. We get extra points for dressing up professionally. I feel so uncomfortable."

Roxxi laughs as she looks him up and down. I begin to feel like a third wheel, so I close my locker and say, "Yeah, you look nice Nick."

Roxxi tears her eyes away from Nick long enough to notice the sad look on my face. "Nick, do you mind giving me a minute to talk to Tamara. This is important," she says as she pulls me towards the bathroom.

"T, what's up? I was out there rambling on about my problems. Never once did I look at you and see the panic and sadness on your face."

"Look at this," I say, lifting my shirt sleeve, and a black and blue bruise is on my arm.

Roxxi gasps in horror at the bruise on my arm. "OMG, Tamara. What happened?"

Just the thought of Kellz putting his hands on me brings me to tears. Tears start to stream down my face. "It was Kellz...he did this to me."

"He hit you?" she asks, sounding at a loss for any other words.

At the same time, my heart drops; I don't want to believe that I've been abused, like some old woman who's dealing with an old jerk too long. I shake my head. "No, but he grabbed me so damn hard that it formed a bruise. He was angry that I wasn't pickin' up the phone!" I sob even louder at the admission of the silly situation that upset Kellz.

Roxxi rubs my shoulder in attempt to comfort me.

"I was so scared, Roxxi. I was literally shaking to the point I couldn't move to check on Tremaine."

Roxxi embraces me in a hug. "Poor thing. You must've been frightened out of your mind. I'm pretty sure you don't know what to think of the situation...or of Kellz. And I don't know whether to be angry or upset myself. But it's going to be okay, T. I'm here for you," Roxxi assures me, and for once I feel at ease. "Does he know that he bruised you?" she asks.

"No. I avoided his phone calls all night."

A few girls start to crowd the bathroom, so we leave out of the restroom and go back to my locker where Chauncey is waiting for me.

"Yo, T, I was looking for you," he says as we approach him. "Hey, Rox."

Roxxi waves, but Chauncey's eyes immediately meet mine. Then, he looks at my bruised arm. "What's that on your arm, Tamara?" he asks, as he embraces me in a hug before giving me a chance to answer.

I brush him off and move away from him. "Don't worry about that, Chauncey. And you might not want to do that. It could only cause more problems," I say as I start to walk away.

"I agree; Kellz could be walking up in any second now. He'll freak the fuck out if he sees Tamara hugging another guy," Roxxi says to Chauncey as a warning.

"What? I'm not scared of your psycho boyfriend...I'm not scared of him. Matter of fact, did he do that to you?" Chauncey asks as he follows us down the hall.

"He didn't mean it," I say, trying to deter him with my glare. I wish he would get the clue and move around. He was good at helping me with my chemistry work. I didn't need him snooping around in my business though.

I look at Roxxi and then back at Chauncey.

"You heard what she said, he didn't mean it," Roxxi says. "Now back off!"

I notice Kellz walking up the hall in our direction, and he doesn't look too happy. Aw hell, I know it's about to be some shit. I'm already upset, and I don't need this right now.

Roxxi jumps in front of me. "Kellz, calm down. I can't allow you to upset T anymore."

Kellz shoves Roxxi out the way and grabs my bruised arm. "We need to talk," he says in a growl.

I snatch my arm away. "I don't feel like talkin' to you right now." He grabs my arm again and I yell, "No Kellz, leave me alone!"

"Kellz stop! She doesn't want to talk to you! Go away!" Roxxi says with a look of horror on her face. "Just leave her alone, please," she begs in my defense.

I begin to sob again, and Chauncey grabs my hand. "Don't cry, beautiful," he says gently looking into my eyes. He then glares at Kellz.

Oh did that add fire to the flame in Kellz's eyes. He grabs Chauncey's shirt and bum rushes him into the lockers.

"Fuck off," Chauncey yells.

"Nigga, I will kill you! Split yo' shit back and won't even blink, lil' nigga. You betta stay on your side of the game before your bitch ass gets dealt with," Kellz says before turning to me. "So you frontin' on me, T! I knew it! You ain't shit! Four years and you start to front on me! Fuck both of yawl!"

With that being said, he pushes Chauncey towards me and marches off down the hallway. The hallway becomes silent as spectators look on. All you can hear are my sniffles and probably the beating of my heart.

I feel sick. I hate for people to see me this way. I don't want Roxxi, who's holding my hand, to feel sorry for me. She looks as if she wants to cry along with me. Chauncey and Roxxi comfort me, but nothing can make me feel better about the man I love storming away after telling me I ain't shit.

* * *

You ain't shit.

I can't concentrate at all in Chemistry class. I just want it to be over. I'm hurting—emotionally, physically, and mentally. Those things that Kellz said to me pierced my soul. It's like he just took a knife and stabbed me with it.

You ain't shit.

Why did he have to take it that far? Honestly, I don't feel like shit.

How could I feel this way about the guy who I gave my heart to? How could I hurt the guy who has done so much for me? I'm such an ungrateful bitch.

Yes you are.

I just want to die.

Lord, please take away this pain! I don't want to live any longer! Why do I have to go through all this bullshit? I just want to be happy, Lord. Why don't you ever answer my prayers? All of a sudden, I begin to feel angry—angry that I suffered for so long! Angry that God allowed me to suffer and that he didn't give a damn about what I was going through! Angry that my mother is never around to comfort me! Angry that my sister never wants to accept her responsibilities. Angry that I now carry her weight on my shoulders! Angry that I love Kellz so much.

Through all my anger, I start to feel a wave of resentment towards Kellz. Got dammit, why can't he ever show me some respect? Why can't he ever call me beautiful? Why can't he get in control of his demons?

I want to scream. I feel my chest burning. I want to let it all out...but luckily the school bell rings, and I rush out of the classroom before I have a full-blown panic attack.

"Tamara! Wait up!" Chauncey shouts at my back.

I pause in my tracks. I wait for him to catch up with me. "You didn't look too good back there," he states the obvious, to which I shrug. "You want to talk about it?"

I shrug again.

"Follow me, Tamara. I want to show you something."

Chauncey grabs my hand and starts to pull me down the hall. When we get to the end of the hallway, we start down the flight of stairs—trying to bum rush the crowd of students heading to their next class. After the flight of stairs, he leads me down another hallway into a double door. He looks both ways to see if anyone is coming before we enter another double door.

"Where are you taking me, Chauncey?" I ask, becoming slightly ambivalent about his impromptu follow-the-leader stunt.

"Just come with me, Tamara, I promise you're safe with me," he says, with his signature smile that puts me at ease.

We walk down another set of stairs which leads us to a dark hallway. No lights. Only one window illuminating the hallway. It's nothing but a wall full of graffiti on both sides of us.

"Um," I murmur. "Are you sure we're supposed to be down here?"

He looks at me. "It's okay. No one ever comes down here."

On our way down the hall, there is a door to our right. After Chauncey opens the door, we walk down some stairs taking us deeper. We stop in an empty room. It smells of dust and old furniture. It's dark and stuffy. Chauncey grabs a lamp and clicks it on.

"Better?" he asks.

I nod my head.

He grabs two chairs from the far corner and motions for me to sit. I don't know what to think. I mean, why are we here, and how the hell did he discover this place?

My shivers are noticeable because it is a lil' chilly. Chauncey notices I'm cold and begins to rub my arms in an attempt to warm me up.

"Welcome to my dungeon," he says. "This is my go-to place when I just want to be alone and let my thoughts loose."

"Wow!" is all I can say.

Wow, in like an amazing way. I don't have a place I can run to when I just want to be alone. I can never be alone. I lost that freedom when I took Tremaine in, not that I regret it, but it would be nice to be at peace sometimes.

"Are you okay, beautiful?" he asks. His eyes gleam from the light. He appears so stress free. So happy with life. I want to be like that.

I look at Chauncey and pause to take in the aura that surrounds him. "Why do you call me that?" I finally get the courage to ask.

"What? Beautiful?"

I nod.

He smiles.

"Because you are."

"No I'm not."

"Like hell you aren't. I love how you're so natural and not artificial like other women. I love how you're not obsessed with materialistic items like other women that go above and beyond to try to look perfect. You have a good spirit. I can feel it. It's sort of natural."

My stomach fills with nervousness and butterflies. No guy has ever deemed me as different or natural. These sweet words he took ownership of make me feel wanted for once. It's a completely different feeling. A feeling I'm really not sure how to deal with.

Kellz has always shown me tough love. I don't know what sweet or romantic feels like, until this moment. My first date with Kellz was at a kickback he and his friends threw in the sixth grade. I was the hostess, and I took the money from the bad-ass hoodlums who self-invited themselves to the kickback. As a matter of fact, it was an open affair to the hood. Anybody from the neighborhood was invited.

All I saw was half naked bitches—bitches I couldn't stand from school—belligerent drunks, and I could smell the thick smoke of weed filling up the room. Later that night, Kellz and I had departed from the event into his bedroom. We were making out, cuddling, and eventually started having sex when we finally had the chance to be alone. That was the night I fell for him.

The things we talked about, the laughs we shared, and the stories we exchanged…There wasn't an angry moment during that time. I felt so comfortable with him. I was blind to the red flags he threw at me. Like the fact that he sold drugs, and he hated school.

I remember him saying it's all about the money, so fuck bitches. Then we'd laugh. Finally he said, "But I can definitely come to love you, shawty. I like how you make a nigga feel."

That's how Kellz always expresses his "sensitivity" towards me. Back then, it made me feel good, but as I have gotten older, I know it's not romantic at all.

"Thank you," I say, finally bringing my thoughts back to the present. "That really does mean a lot. That was sweet."

Chauncey grabs my hand and kisses it. His lips are soft, and his touch sends a chill down my body. "And that's what you deserve. I hated to see you cry. You don't deserve that."

I stare into his eyes and melt. "Do I really deserve so many kind words from you?" I ask, still unsure of his motive, not ready to trust the feeling of confidence growing in my gut.

"Yes, beautiful."

We lock eyes for a few more seconds. He leans in towards me. My mind is telling me that I should pull back, but my heart is telling me the opposite.

As our lips lock, the magic I felt with Kellz I begin to feel with Chauncey. Only this time, it's a little sweeter. So sweet, I go in for another kiss. The magic sparkles, and I don't want it to end.

Chapter 13

KELLZ

It's ten at night, and I pull up to the strip club. It's ducked off in the cut, and there aren't a lot of cars in the parking lot. I notice two security guards standing at the entrance. Although I'm still pissed at what happened today with Tamara, I can't let it stop the flow of my money.

At least I don't have to step foot into that damn school for the next two weeks. Somebody snitched on me for my behavior in the hallway, which got me suspended for two weeks. They just don't know they did me a fuckin' favor 'cause I decided I'm not goin' back at all.

I bet you it was that bitch-nigga Tamara messing with that snitched on me. Fuck them both! I ain't never been so hurt in my life, but of course I won't let any bitch or nigga see me sweat. She'll come running back. No doubt. Imma just give her time...maybe.

I take a deep breath and glance at the club one more time before departing from the car. As I approach the guards, I put on my game face and make sure my pistol tucked to where they can't find it if they were to search a nigga.

"Aye, I'm here to see J-Money."

"Is that right?" the guard with the eye patch says. "You got a weapon on you?"

"Nah."

The guards look at each other and laugh.

"This nigga here," the other one says. "Who you think you foolin' kid? Hand it over. You can get it back when you leave."

I step up to the guards. "I said I ain't got shit."

The guards laugh again like I'm some damn comedian.

"Oh, we got a tough one on our hands, Lavern."

"It's cool. He ain't gon' last long," the guard with the eye patch, Lavern, says.

"What kind of name is Lavern? Fuck both of yawl lames. Let me in." I try to walk past them, but the guards yank me back.

Lavern places me in a headlock. "The fuck. You young niggas gon' learn some got damn respect! You ain't entering until you hand over the weapon!"

Before I can retaliate, Lavern pushes me to the ground and places his boot on my chest. As he presses down on my chest, it becomes hard for me to breathe.

"You got three seconds kid. One—two—"

"Okay," I manage to say. "Fuck!" I reach in my pants and pull out my Glock. I can't let these clowns fuck with my money. The other guard snatches the gun out of my hands as Lavern helps me off the ground.

"Aiight. You can go in."

I straighten myself before I enter the doors of the club, giving both guards a look as I enter the doors. It's dark inside the club except for the strobe lights flashing everywhere. Rap music is blasting from every wall, and the smell of smoke fills the air of the building.

I turn my head towards the bar and notice this chick lookin' at me. She looks like she's bartending. She's wearing some cut-off booty shorts with a small t-shirt that barely covers her boobs. She has red hair that stops just above her thick ass. I notice how tatted she is, with ink covering almost her entire body, and the lip and belly piercings she has. I'll admit, shawty is bad as hell, but she don't concern me. Can't trust these bitches no way.

She smiles and waves for me to come over. I think nawl, but my feet begin to make my way over there. "What's up," I say as I approach her.

"You tell me. I noticed you as you walked in. Thought I'd speak."

I nod. "Word? I didn't know I turned heads when I walked in a room."

"Apparently so, sexy. So whatchu drinking?"

"What you got strong?"

"Oooo," she says. "You are a dare devil huh? Maybe a shot of Patron?"

"Only if you take a shot with me."

She smiles. "Aiight. You got it."

As she prepares the shots, I glance at her body. I'm surprised she isn't a stripper. She has the body for it. And the look. She has the look of a freak and a bad girl, and that turns me on. I like how she looks exotic and voluptuous at the same time. "You got a man?" I ask.

She looks at me and smirks. "Nah."

"How about we make it plural. Any men?" I smile so she can sense that I'm being humorous, but really I'm dead ass.

She shakes her head. "Nah. Just me."

"Yeah right."

"Whatever. I know you have an old lady at home. I know who you are—Kellz."

"Damn. Where you know me from?"

"My cousin is your homeboy...Shad."

I gasp. "Damn! For real? What's your name, shawty?"

"Sha'tila."

"Mmm. Nice to meet you Sha'tila."

She places my shot in front of me. "Same to you. Drink up."

We both tilt our heads to intake the shots, and I notice how alcohol doesn't phase me anymore. Hell, I drunk so much growing up, it's almost like juice to me.

"Well, you took that well," she says laughing. "You think you can call me sometime, Kellz? I need a drinkin' partner."

"Maybe I can take you up on that offer. Maybe not. You smoke?"

"Of course. Gotta have my stress reliever."

"Now you talkin," I say. "Maybe we can smoke sometime."

She nods, then writes her number on a piece of paper. "Maybe this weekend. Just hit me up."

I stare at the paper and then look back at her. "Aiight. Um, do you know where I can find J-Money?"

"Of course. He's been waiting for you. Follow me."

She leads me to the back of the club, away from the scene, to a rusted kitchen door. From there, she leads me down a tiny hallway, down some stairs, and we stop at a solid wooden door. She knocks until a voice commands us to enter. She opens the door and motions for me to enter.

"Thanks," I say to her before she walks away, and I'm greeted by J-Money, who is propped behind a solid cherry wood desk with his feet kicked up.

"Kellz! My boy...you made it."

"Yup, when money calls...I come."

"I like that, Kellz. I really, really like that."

J-Money sits up in his chair and motions for me to take a seat. He offers me a cigar, but I turn it down. Ain't no tellin' what he laced it with. Plus, I'm trying to get out of here quick, fast in a hurry. His office is fuckin wit' my nostrils. It reeks of sour-smelling ass, musk, and cigar smoke.

"Sooo," I start off slowly. "What's up? Why am I here?"

"For one thing...I want you to work for me. You do what you suppose to do. You get paid and live the life you deserve. Whatcha' think?"

I pause for a moment. "How much you talkin'?"

"You can bring in at least five to ten G's a week. Maybe more...it all depends on you."

The numbers damn sho' sound good. I'm just trying to decide if I want to be down with him.

"We just have one rule," he adds.

"What's that?"

"Loyalty. No snitchin' allowed. Meaning no snitchin' on your fellow brothers and no ratting to the cops who you work for. If you do so, severe consequences will be brought into action."

I shrug. If it's one thing I got, it's loyalty. I ain't ever snitched to no pigs and don't ever plan to, so it's with certainty that I say, "Sure. What else you got?"

J-Money chuckles. "Ah my boy ready to put in that work."

"Yeah, I'm ready to get to this money," I say in all seriousness.

"Slow your roll, rookie. Imma get you there. You familiar with the drug business—in which I'm pretty sure you are considering your brother slayed on some corners. He had it down packed. I need you to be like your brother. Less talkin', more doin'. As a matter of fact, how is he?"

For some reason, I feel a spark of rage go through my chest. I don't like to talk about Terrell. I haven't visited him in over a month. Prolly 'cause I'm too ashamed. I swear he wanted me to be different. That's why he took the blame for that murder.

He wanted me to change my life around. Those tears he shed as they placed him behind the cop car as I watched from a distance, the hurt, the pain that was drawn on his face stung my heart like a bee. Shit still hurts 'til this day.

I guess J-Money read the look on my face. He apologizes for bringing the subject to light. "I know it's tough for you...but work for me. Then maybe I can pull some strings and I can get him out. Its ways around this shitty-ass system. I know people."

I glare at him. "Don't fuck with me about my brother, J-Money."

"I'm not. I swear I can make it happen for you—everything. What do you say?"

My mind is racing, but I never take my eyes off J-Money. That would be my biggest dream—to get Terrell out of jail. I have always pushed that dream to the side. I don't know if I can trust this motherfucker, but I damn sure like the promises he's making me. He just better pray that they aren't false promises, or his life will be fucked up.

"Let's do this shit then..." I finally say.

Chapter 14

ROXXI

I'm so glad the school day is over. My friends were acting weird. All Tamara could talk about was Chauncey during lunch. We didn't see Kellz around that whole day, and Tamara never mentioned one word about him. When I did ask her about him, she just shrugged and kept blabbing about Chauncey. Then, I saw Nick conversing with his ex, and when I got to arguing with her in the middle of the hallway, he called me immature and walked off.

The rest of the day, he didn't utter no more than two words to me. I just wanted to go home and sulk in my bed for the entire night. I slick wanted to cry, but no tears left my eyes.

Finally, I reach home and feel a sense of relief, but my heart sinks when I see my mother on the kitchen floor with blood running down her legs.

"Mom!" I scream as I rush to her side.

I feel for a pulse. Thank God, she has a pulse. But she's unconscious.

"Oh my god! Oh my god!" I yell.

My mind is racing, and my heart is pounding. I'm too scared to figure out what to do next. *Just call 911, Roxxi!* I pull my cell phone out of my purse and hurriedly dial 911. I'm too emotional to talk, so the operator repeatedly asks me questions.

I manage to say, "Sh-sh-she's unconscious! Sh-sh-she's bleeding! Sh-sh-she's pregnant! Please hurry!"

"What's your address ma'am?"

"201 Windsgate Drive, hurry!" I repeat again becoming impatient.

"An ambulance is on its way," states the operator.

After I hang up with 911, I immediately call my stepdad. I take a wet towel and begin to wipe the blood from my mother's legs. I tremble and sob with every wipe.

The fight we had begins to replay in my head. I didn't mean for it to go down like this. My heart begins to pound harder, and suddenly I can't breathe. My stomach quivers, and I throw up; the guilty feelings inside of me are making me sick.

"I'm sorry, Mom," I whisper as I caress her cheek. "I'm sorry..." I hold her hand throughout the whole ride to the hospital.

Chapter 15

NICKHOLAS

It's pushing ten o'clock when Roxxi calls with the news that her mom is in the hospital after a bad fall. I can barely understand what Roxxi's saying through her tears and sobs. She blames herself for what happened. I reassure her it's only an accident...not a coincidence.

I need to be there to comfort my girl. I want to be there...but I have no wheels yet. While we're on the phone, Vanessa keeps beeping through the line.

A sudden noise down the stairs interrupts my call. "Rox, babe, believe this if you don't believe anything else; everything will be okay with your mom. Listen, I'll hit you back later, okay?" I say.

"Thanks, Nick. Talk to you soon," she says before hanging up.

Who the fuck? I think as I creep downstairs and notice the back door is open.

Oh my god! Somebody is trying to fuckin' rob us!

I reach for the nearest object, which happens to be my mother's umbrella. I keep creeping to the kitchen where I hear our refrigerator door being opened. This a hungry-ass burglar. Must be a joke.

"Aye nigga!" I quickly switch on the kitchen lights to alert the burglar. I'm relieved to find that it is only Kellz.

"Brah, what the fuck you gon' do wit' a umbrella?" he says with a mouth full of grapes.

I drop the umbrella on the floor and sigh. "Dude. You scared me shitless. How in the hell did you get through the back door?"

He grabs a whole bag of Doritos and begins to munch on them. "Devon let me in."

"Hungry much?"

Kellz nods. "Hell yeah. Yawl barely got shit though. The fuck."

"So you're going to eat our food and talk shit too?" I say, shaking my head.

"Yeah, man' yawl needa go shopping. But braaaahhh, I gotta tell you about this baddie I met at the strip club. Her name is Sha'tila. Shawty wanna smoke wit' me. Then I got this new gig bringing in five G's or more a week. Not to mention ol' dude said he can pull some ties to get Terrell outta jail."

I'm taken back by all the news my boy is laying on me. Terrell is in jail for murder. Do he really think someone can pull strings on his case? Kellz walks into the living room still spilling information as I follow.

"So what about Tamara?" I ask.

He flops on the couch, throws a chip in his mouth, and looks at me. "Apparently she gotta thang for wimpy-ass niggas. She dogged me the other day."

"So are you two not together?"

He shrugs. "Don't know. I know one thing: that nigga gotta ass whoopin' coming tho. Fuck 'em both."

"Aye! Watch your language, young man!" a booming, deep voice says. I jump when I seen my dad appear at the bottom of the stairs.

"My bad, pops," Kellz says.

"What are you doing here anyways, boy? Don't you have a home?"

"Nope. Moms kicked me out."

Dad walks over to the couch to get a better view of Kellz before he proceeds with his questioning. "And why in the hell is that?"

"She found weed in my room."

"You actually smoke that shit?" my dad asks.

Kellz nods.

Dad looks at me, and I quickly turn my head. I mean, I'm not an avid smoker, but I have hit a blunt a few times. Dad starts to shake his head.

"Boy I tell ya'. I don't know what's wrong with you young boys. Ya' steady throwing your lives away."

Kellz quickly closes the bag of chips. "You don't know shit I have to go through, so don't sit here and lecture me." He stands up to leave, and I wish my dad would just shut his ass up.

103

"Sit your ass down, boy! That's your problem! You think you know everything! Kellz, the tough shit who swear he can beat everybody's ass! Don't play that tough shit with me! See I was you a looong time ago, and I swear my life was almost ruined! Trust me, I've been through worse son. Homeless, uneducated, starving, and angry. Then, I started to hustle, but that shit led to more problems. Drama, lies, deceit, more pain and anger. I was a lost soul."

"Well, this who I am. I can't change that," Kellz states with meaning.

"But is it who you are destined to be? Kellz, anybody can change...I did," my dad says.

It becomes awkwardly quiet in the room. I clear my throat to present some noise.

"Can I sleep here tonight?" Kellz finally asks.

Dad lets out a breath. "Go ahead, but don't make this a habit. Get your shit together son."

When pop disappears upstairs, I ask if Kellz is okay. He blankly stares at the wall and nods. "I'm cool."

In a way, I'm glad my father had this talk with him. He needed to hear it. Will it get through to him? I don't know, but it brought some type of emotion from him. I can read it on his face.

"Well, goodnight dude. See you in the morning," I say, going to bed with hopes that my nigga would change.

Chapter 16

KELLZ

The talk from pops has a nigga's mind on a hundred. But I can't let it get in the way of my mission this Friday morning. I pull up to the school just as everyone is changing classes. Even though I'm suspended, I get out and walk into the building heading straight for Tamara's locker.

I have something in store for that nigga Chauncey. I have to get my revenge on him for turning Tamara against me. I'm too turnt up when I see his punk ass standing at Tamara's locker. Both of them laughing as if he's really funny.

I notice the biggest grin on Tamara's face as she laughs at something he says. When I walk up, the laughing stops, and Tamara looks down at the ground.

"What's so funny? Damn T, I haven't heard from you in a couple days. I guess you're preoccupied, huh?" I look at Chauncey. "I guess you like taking a nigga's girl? You're just that charming, huh?" Neither of them speak back. "Damn. Are yawl lost for words? Wasn't expecting to see me here, huh?"

"Back off," Chauncey finally says, doing exactly what I wanted him to do—challenge me.

"Back off, you say?" I ask as I quickly swing my fist back and land a right hook on that nigga's face.

Tamara screams, "Stop it Kellz!"

Chauncey falls to the ground, and I continue to throw blows at his head and face while yelling, "Fuck nigga! Whassup now! Huh! Whassup?"

Tamara grabs my shirt, and I throw her off me. Then, I grab Chauncey's shirt and lift him off the ground. Nigga's whole face is covered in blood. He's barely conscious.

I throw his body towards Tamara as the whole hallway watches in fear.

"Talk that shit now, nigga!"

I'm so got damn angry. The only bitch I trusted turned her back on me. After all the shit I've done for her. All the laughs we shared. All the love we made.

I glare at her. My loyalty...my pride...my heart...my soul.

She's so busy trying to hold Chauncey up that she doesn't notice my glare—my angry glare. It takes so much for me not to slap her ass in her face too, but my work is done.

"I hope you're happy, Tamara," I say before walking off.

Not even ten minutes later, I'm called into Principal Mahone's office. Mr. Charles, the school's security guard, had caught me as I was walking back out to my car, and he led me to the office.

As I take a seat, I feel relieved knowing that I'm about to get more time out of school, on top of my two week suspension. I have no problem getting away from this place. The only reason I'm here now is because I had to deal with Chauncey.

"Mr. Smith, why am I not surprised to see you here?" he begins.

"Just add some days to my suspension and I'm out."

"Suspension? You're on the borderline of being expelled. I don't think this school can take any more of your crap. You damn near knocked the boy into a coma. If commanded, charges will be pressed against you. We're waiting for Chauncey's dad now. Do you have anything to say for yourself, young man?

I chuckle. "Nope. Expulsion is even better."

Principal Mahone stares at me with a straight face.

"I'm glad you think that this is funny, Mr. Smith—"

"Not funny, hilarious," I say as I laugh even harder.

Mr. Charles chimes in, "Do you not care about school?"

I shake my head. "Nope. Gives not one fuck. Plus, I gotta good job. I ain't worried about this corrupted educational system...I ain't worried 'bout nuttin'! Learning what a X mean in algebra ain't gonna get me nowhere."

"Selling weed doesn't count as good money, Mr. Smith," Mr. Charles says.

"Pssh. Let you tell it."

Principal Mahone places his hands on the back of his head and leans back in his chair. "Fine. You want to be expelled? Then you got it."

"Come on, Mahone. Don't expel the boy. You and I both know he needs to be here, even if he has to stay back. He just needs the proper guidance."

"What?" I retort.

"I think it's pretty clear that he's not serious about being here, so why keep him here? Just one less student to worry about."

"First of all, as you being a part of the educational system, those foul words should not be coming out of your mouth. Your job is to lead this school and to be a leader. Your job is to help make sure these students are learning and striving to become better people so when they get out into the real world, life won't be such a challenge to them. No student should be left behind!"

"Mr. Charles I—"

"Look, just hold the boy back if you have to, but don't expel him."

"Expel me," I say, wishing Mr. Charles would shut up with this no-one-left-behind crap.

"Hush boy!" Mr. Charles says to me and then turns his attention back to Principal Mahone. "Look, I will take him under my wing, and he will try again."

"No," I yell. "Fuck that!"

"Hush," Mr. Charles yells back.

Principle Mahone sits up and lets out a breath.

"Well, if charges are not pressed, the boy may stay, but he will be suspended for the next month, which is going to cause him to miss the graduation test. So he will have to repeat the classes he has failed, some of which are offered this summer along with graduation tutoring classes. But if charges are pressed, the boy will be expelled. Deal?"

"Hell no," I chime in.

"Yes, Mr. Mahone. It's a deal."

"Okay. Mr. Smith, you are dismissed from the school's premises until further notice."

"He ain't my daddy! He can't command shit," I say about Mr. Charles.

"Mr. Smith," Mr. Mahone yells. "I am done with this conversation. You are dismissed."

I storm out of his office, infuriated at the shit that just happened.

"I'm just trying to save you boy," Mr. Charles says as he follows me out into the hallway.

"Your old ass can't save me. I don't need you to feel sorry for me. I don't need your help!"

"You're going to regret not getting your diploma."

"I gives no fucks about some shitty-ass piece of paper, man."

"Well you better start. I only want to help you. You're on a path of destruction, and I just want to help...my son died from staying out in the streets four years ago, and it still hurts my heart till this day. Before he died, he told me he wanted to get his life together, then those hoodlums shot him.

They still haven't found who murdered my son. They left his body laying lifeless inside of a dumpster." He paused. "I promised myself that I would save any young brother who was heading down that same path, just to save his life."

"I'm good," I say with stubborn pride.

"Please. Please, let me help you. God won't let me rest until I do. Do you have a place to stay? Have you taken a shower? Are you hungry?"

"Like I said, I don't need you to feel sorry for me. My father ain't feel sorry for me when he just up and left, so I don't need no other man feeling sorry for me."

"I'm not feeling sorry for you. I just want to help. Give you a roof over your head and food to eat. I'm going to talk to Chauncey and his dad to try and change their minds if they press charges. Do you need a lift?"

"Nope. I gotta whip."

Mr. Charles pulls out a small notepad and a pen and starts to write on it. "Well, if you want to take me up on that offer, just come by the crib. I'll be there, son."

He hands me the piece of paper and walks off. I crumble it up. I place the paper in my jeans pocket after realizing sleeping in a bed and taking a hot shower would do a nigga justice. I know I'm supposed to leave the school's premises, but I can't leave just yet.

Chapter 17

TAMARA

I glance at Chauncey and immediately feel so bad for him. His whole face is puffy with both eyes swollen shut. His lip is twice as big as normal, and he can barely speak. The nurse cleans him up a bit, and we wait for his dad and the ambulance to take him to the hospital.

I am infuriated! I'm so mad I pray to God that his dad presses charges on Kellz. A few tears roll down my face. "I'm so sorry, Chauncey."

Mrs. Grier, the nurse, gives me permission to go back to class. "I will notify you if anything changes, Tamara."

I nod, barely having the energy to speak. "Ok," is all I say.

How could Kellz be so selfish and stupid?

Oh right, it's in his nature.

It's tearing me up inside that it ended like this. What if Chauncey never wants to speak to me again? What if he is scared for his life? What if he decides to not tutor me anymore? I swear if Kellz prevents me from walking across the stage, I will never forgive him!

I stop to punch the locker and let off some steam.

"I guess I'm not the only one that's mad," a voice says. I turn around and feel disgusted.

"Leave me alone, Kellz. You've done enough today."

He grabs my hand. "Is this really how you feel? Is this really how you're going to do me after—"

"Shut up," I yell. "Get over yourself! You are so fucked up 'til the point you don't even know the damage you are causing towards everyone around you! Your friends...your family—everyone. I'm so sick of your shit, Kellz. Your anger, your attitude, and your demeanor."

"Fuck that," he yells back. "You are supposed to be the only one who has my back. But you turned on me just like everyone else. What a bitchy thing for you to do! Was Chauncey there when you were going through hell and back? No! I was there! Does he help with Tremaine? No! I do! You don't know how bad a nigga is hurting, brah. I fuckin' loved yo fuck ass, but you turned on me."

I weep. His words stab me like a knife, and it goes deeper with every word. "Kellz, I can't do this," I whisper.

"What part of it you can't do? Because you seem to be doing a lot these days," he says.

"I can't do this with you anymore. I will forever love you, but I'm broken inside. I—"

"Ah man, T! Nooo...Nooo! You breakin' up wit a nigga! After four years?" Kellz's eyes begin to water, but he holds back any tears from falling. This only makes me cry harder.

He becomes quiet, and the look on his face is distant. "I'm sorry I hurt you..." he says as he turns to leave.

I want to scream for him. I want to give him a hug. I want to wipe the tears from his face. Suddenly, my anger turns into hurt. What if I'm making a huge mistake? I love this man! What's best for me?

The feeling of hatred towards my life appears all over again as I begin to feel sick to my stomach. I just don't want to live anymore. I am a confused soul in a big world. I have no plans. No goals. No money. No boyfriend. I fuck everything up. I run to the bathroom before I vomit all over the hallway floor. Maybe I am the problem? Not Kellz.

Where did all this courage to really tell him how I feel come from? I gag until my throat begins to burn. All I need is a hug right now, but I have no one to turn to. I just want to crawl to my bed and stay there forever, but of course I can't do that. I have a kid at home.

I take a deep breath. I really need to get myself on the right track. I mean, Kellz did do a lot for me. Now I have to learn to do for myself. It's the only way my son and I can survive.

Gotta stop feeling sorry for yourself, girl. You can do this...without Kellz.

I pull myself together, stuffy nose and all. I force a quick smile on my lips then head to class doubting that voice in my head.

Chapter 18

TAMARA

"Rox, I've had so much personal drama going on, I forgot to ask you how was your brother," I say, feeling completely horrible for only thinking about myself and not what my friend was going through. It has been a few days since the big fight with Chauncey and Kellz. Since Chauncey got released from the hospital, I've been making sure he's comfortable and helping around the house. I told his parents I would do anything to help out since it was my psychotic boyfriend—ex-boyfriend—who caused this whole thing.

"Oh, he's fine. He was born premature, but he's going to be okay," she says, bringing me back to the present.

We're walking through the halls in between classes. I feel like other students are accusing me with their eyes as they glance at me. So I just focus on my friend...the only one that matters. "The fall was so fatal that if he had stayed inside her, he would have choked on the blood, so they had to cut him out. My mom seemed depressed the whole time she was in the hospital," she adds.

"I'm just glad everyone is okay. Have you and your mom made up about your fight?"

"When she got home, her mood lightened up a little. She was still kind of stressed because the hospital had to keep the baby to make sure he didn't have any more complications. It wasn't until the baby was released to come home that she began to act like her normal self. We made up and made a promise not to ever fight like that again." Roxxi is all smiles as she talks about her improved relationship with her mother. I'm happy for her.

"Well, that's good to hear. At least one of us is happy."

"It feels good to get our relationship back on track," she admits. "And my baby brother's smile can warm up your heart, and I love to poke his dimples."

"I can't wait to come see him," I say.

"Yeah...Have you talked to Kellz since the fight?"

"No, and I don't plan to. I was hoping they would lock him up after what he did to Chauncey. Unfortunately, Chauncey and his parents didn't press charges after talking to the principal."

"How could you say that about Kellz? You are his world. He needs you, T. Why would you throw it all away?" She stops and looks at me as if she's trying to understand me.

"Kellz has been acting like a mad man, and I'm not going to let him treat me any kind of way," I say, remembering the crazed look Kellz had on his face the night he grabbed me by the arm.

"Are you sure it's not the fact that you hooked up with Chauncey? You know he fought him because he was angry about how things were going between you two."

"But that doesn't make it right," I say, becoming upset about her constant nagging.

"T, you need to think about this, very closely. Even you have always said Kellz has been good to you."

"Will you just shut the hell up and leave me alone about it! Go back to your perfect little boyfriend and your perfect fucking life and stay out my business!" I cringe as soon as the words leave my mouth. Roxxi is too shocked to even say anything back to me. She just walks away.

After school, I head home to check on Tremaine. Surprisingly, my mother is at home, and she agrees to keep Tremaine while I drive her car to Chauncey's house. His mother lets me in, and I help her with a few chores before going into the living room to have a seat.

I haven't spoken to Roxxi since our argument at school earlier today. I'm a little upset at myself for slumping down to this emotional state. It's like I dug a hole for myself. The more I try to climb out of it, the more my darkened emotions want me to stay.

God, just save me by killing me now. I don't care how you do it. Just kill me now.

"Baby, are you okay?"

I turn to see that Chauncey made his way out of bed into the living room where I was sitting contemplating my life. I sniffle "Yeah, I'm fine. What are you doing here?"

"This is my house, babe," he says as he sits next to me. Although I want to smile at his sarcasm, I can't find that emotion in myself.

117

"I mean, what are you doing out of bed? I thought you were sleep."

"Can't sleep. I'm worried about you."

He grabs my hand to place in his and kisses it.

I'm silent until I finally have the courage to speak. "I'm so sorry, Chauncey." I begin to let my tears flow because I can no longer hold them in.

"Awl, babe. For what? It's not your fault." He wipes the tears from my face and embraces me in a hug. "If you want me to, I can decide to press charges. If that'll make you feel better."

I snatch away from his embrace and shoot him a dirty look. "No, he's going to get what he deserves," I say quietly. I look down at the floor and really want this conversation to be over.

"Uhhh, that was a very interesting reaction. You..." he pauses. "Nothing. Never mind."

"What Chauncey?"

I look at him to express my concern, and he just rolls his eyes.

"Forget it. Clearly you switched up, and now you want to defend the guy."

"If you wanted to press charges, then you should have done it in the first place. There's no reason to jump up and do it now. Give it a got damn break, will ya?" I bury my face in my hands and let out more sobs.

"Look, I'm sorry Tamara. I know you are going through the motions right now. I'm here for you."

He rubs his hand up and down my back to express his want to comfort me. It just isn't comforting enough. I'm an emotional wreck. I should feel slightly embarrassed for allowing him to see me this way. I've never cried so much in front of someone, not even Kellz.

Am I being punished for something I've done? All I want is to finally be happy, and I don't know if Chauncey can do that part...I mean, I have to get myself in order.

"I'm sorry. I just really need to get myself together. My life. Just everything."

"You will. Just give it time."

I shake my head. "You don't understand. I have a son to raise. I need to get my own place. I need to graduate. I need to attend someone's college. I need money. I need—"

"You need someone who can actually help you and give you the push you need. I'm that guy for you. I'll do anything to make sure all your goals and dreams happen for you, T. Just trust me." Chauncey pokes out his lips signaling his kissy face.

I let out a slight laugh and peck his lips. "I just don't know what to do first. I'm so overwhelmed."

"Well, testing is a couple weeks away. So we can start with that, and we can talk about getting you a job. Do you have a resume?"

I shake my head, no.

"Cool. We can also start with that." He flashes me a smile, and I begin to warm up to his loving company.

"Thank you."

"Really. It's not a problem, T."

I don't know how drastic my life is going to change now that Kellz is out of the picture, but I hope it changes for the better. It just has to.

Chapter 19

NICKHOLAS

I am bored out of my mind. I am so tired of repeating the same math problems over and over until I want to throw my math book out the damn window.

It's for graduation though, Nick. Gotta do it.

There is a knock on my bedroom door, and my pop appears in the doorway.

"Yo, what's up pops?"

"Hey. Did you know we had neighbors moving in next door?"

I shake my head. "Nope. But that's dope!"

"Yeah, they are moving in now. Seem like nice people."

"Cool." It is silent.

"Hey son, I really want to speak about the whole Kellz situation—"

"Pops, it's okay," I say, getting up from my bed. "He needed to hear it."

"Yeah...listen. Are you...you know...smoking weed or selling it?"

I laugh. "No pops."

"Have you tried it?"

"Of course." It becomes quiet again. "But you don't have to worry about me pops. I'm not into it like that. No matter who my friends are."

Pops forms a slight smile. "Good because Kellz is a bad influence and..." his voice trails off.

"Dad, I can handle myself. I'm a big boy." I pat pops on the shoulders then head downstairs to peep out the neighbors.

I spot a shiny black Chrysler 300 next to a white Range Rover and a huge U-Haul truck. Damn they stuntin'. Gotta be packing with some money. A tall, light skin, curly hair man walks toward the U-Haul with a boy who looks around the age of Devon following him. Must be father and son.

The dad looks like he's packing with money. I bet that boy is spoiled as hell—just like Devon. I think about introducing myself. Shiid, I wanna be just like that man. Fly as shit. I can tell by the crease in his tan pants he's a top boss. I turn to walk towards the kitchen, but suddenly a pretty little thang catches my attention. My jaw drops. "Damn she fine!" I say, as I stare at shorty.

She stands about five feet five inches with a face so gorgeous and a flawless body. Her skin is a mocha color, and she has long, black, curly hair. She looks like something from the front of a magazine. Suddenly my mind goes blank, and before you know it I'm making my way over to there.

"Oh hey there," she greets as soon as she sees me approaching her way.

"Hey...Uh, I know this is awkward, but I just came to introduce myself to you and your folks."

She flashes me a smirk, and her green eyes look me up and down. "Mmm," she says.

"Mmm," I say back. We just stare at each other until her dad interrupts our play.

She's digging my looks too.

"Hey. You are....?" her dad asks.

"Nick." I snap out of my trance and hold out my hand for him to shake it.

"Nice to meet you," he says, returning the gesture. "I'm Mr. Campbell. This is my daughter Amaria and my son AJ. My wife's in the house unpacking some boxes."

"Okay cool. Welcome to the neighborhood. I had no idea anyone was moving in."

"Yeah, it was sort of a last minute thing. So, your dad told me you play basketball. Interested in playing on a team?"

"As a matter of fact I am, sir. I'm going to join my college basketball team."

"Oh yeah? Interested in playing for the summer?"

"Uhhh...heck yeah."

"Cool. We should talk later."

I nod my head. "Most definitely, sir."

When Amaria and I are alone again, the staring contest begins.

"Mmm," she says.

"Mmm," I say back.

"Aren't you just the sexiest thing?"

I smile. "I could say the same for you."

She does a playful shrug. "You think so?"

"Hell yeah." I bite my lip to show her that I want her bad already. "You're exotic lookin," I say.

"Yup. I get that all the time. My mom is white and Korean. My dad is black, Indian, and Puerto Rican."

"I can dig it. You single?"

She laughs. "Why? You thinking about pursuing me?"

"Shiid if you let me, ma."

She laughs again. "I only fucks with the best."

"I'm the best there is."

"Oh yeah? Is that your Escalade?"

I look back to see my dad's precious baby parked in the driveway with the sunlight reflecting off the rims. By the best, this chick must mean ballers, and that's not me.

"Ye-yeah. I, uh, my dad bought it for me like a year ago. That's my baby."

"Nice," she replies. "That's my baby over there." She points to the white Range Rover. "It was a gift."

"Yeah. You ride in mine, I ride in yours?" She lifts her eyebrow.

"Of course. Then we can race to see which is the fastest." I smirk.

"You're a lil' dare devil aren't you?" She smiles, and we stare at each other once more.

"Amaria! Your mother wants you now," her father calls.

She sighs before speaking again. "God, I hate moving! Well...Nick...we should hang out sometime. Let's say this Saturday...like a movie and dinner? Your treat?"

I nod as I watch her walk away in her fitted shorts that hug her hips and ass just right. As I'm walking back into the house, it dawns on me that I had promised to hang with Roxxi this Saturday.

Shit!

I can't be in two places at once. I have to cancel with one of these females. I mean, Roxxi is my bae...but damn Amaria is irresistible. Maybe I can reschedule with Roxxi....Just maybe.

Chapter 20

KELLZ

I hold the gun to my temple with my finger on the trigger. Tears begin to roll down a nigga's face, and I just want to forget about the chain of unfortunate events that has been happening in my life. First I lost my brother, and then I lost my girl. The only two people I kept fighting for. The only reasons why I wanted to keep living.

I feel sweat drop down my forehead. I look around one last time to make sure no one is walking up to my car. I close my eyes, and I pull the trigger. *POW!* A nigga was depressed.

I really wanted to pull the trigger that night, but something stopped me.

A week had passed, and all I can think about is it is all that nigga Chauncey's fault! If he hadn't of come into the picture, I would still have my bae. Or was she feeling this way for a long time and was scared to break up with a nigga?

All I know is, I seem so small without Tamara. No phone calls. No text messages. No arguments. No crying Tremaine. I couldn't even wipe her tears anymore.

I could tell her I love her, but would she say it back? I pull out my phone and begin to ponder on that thought. After five minutes, I decide against it.

Fuck it! She ain't worried 'bout a nigga no way! Fuck her! Why the fuck am I depressed over a bitch that was willing to throw four years of loyalty away for a motherfucka she just met two months ago?

I glance up to see a black Dodge Charger slowly passing by with some nigga hanging out the window of the passenger side beamin' his eyes at me.

"What the fuck you lookin' at, busta?" I yell, and the car just speeds off. "Yeah you betta take off bitch," I mumble under my breath. Then a white Escalade parks beside me, and I start to think I'm being set up until Nick hops out of it. I get out the car to dap my nigga and show some brotherly love.

"Why are we here at this raggedy-ass strip club?"

"Cause I need you to ride with me to handle some business—ya know—just in case."

"In case of what?"

"Trouble."

Nick pauses in his footsteps.

"Oh no, no, no Kellz," he says. "I don't want any trouble!"

I smack my teeth and look at him. Pussy.

"Will you chill? You have nun to worry 'bout. We get in; we get out. Simple as that, brah. Now let's go," I say.

Once in the club, I'm greeted with a hug from Sha'tila. I'm slick happy to see her. She looks sexy as hell. We've been texting lately, but never had our smoke session yet. I was too busy running up behind Tamara.

"We still need to have our smoke session, Miss Lady."

She nods and then smiles. "We sure do...I'm free Saturday.

"We can get as high as we want," I laugh.

"No doubt."

Nick clears his throat signaling that he wants to be introduced to my new boo—yeah my new boo.

"Oh. This my boy Nick. Nick this is Sha'tila." They shake hands.

"I heard so much about you," Nick says.

She blushes. "Really?"

I nudge Nick in his stomach to shut him up. "I'll talk to you later, shawty."

"Okay boo," she says with a sweet smile.

I lead Nick to J-Money's office. I am ready to get on the job.

"Ah Kellz...and a friend," J-Money says by way of a greeting. "What's up?"

"Yeah, I hope you don't mind. He's following me tonight," I say.

"I'm not responsible for extra niggas. You know that, right?"

"Shit, you ain't responsible for me either. So let's get this shit started," I say.

We take a seat in front of J-Money's desk as we wait for the instructions. J-Money takes a long puff out of his cigar then blows the smoke towards us.

"Well, I have two stops for you to make tonight. One of them being of high priority. First one is really just to make sure I receive my two G's from Kemp. The second stop, you're going to visit a great friend of mine." He smirks. "Brah owes me over a hunnad thou and a duffle bag of...stuff. It's been over two weeks, and I still haven't seen his face. His location is off of Broad Street...south from here. And when you see him, I want no words. All action. Got that?"

"You mean kill him?" Nick asks.

"Nawl, just scare and shake him up a little. If you don't come back with what he owes me, then I'll do the dirty work."

"Cool. Let's go Nick."

"Wait. Make sure you're protected." J-Money reaches into his desk drawer and pulls out a nine millimeter.

I shake my head. "Already have one."

J-Money offers it to Nick.

Nick looks at me and back at J-Money. "Oh nawl. I'm good. Won't be needed."

"What? Take the gun. Just in case," I say.

"No, I'm not leaving my fingerprints on that shit!" Nick says.

I can't believe he's acting like such a pussy. "Fool, you don't have to use it! It's in case of an emergency!"

"You got me fucked up," he says, raising his voice. "I'm not with this dumb shit." Nick storms off, leaving a sharp cringe of anger in my chest.

When I catch up with him, I ask, "What's your got damn problem?"

"I don't want no part of this, and you shouldn't either! Our lives—your life is at stake here. You don't know these people! You think you know the game, but you don't. You think you can solve everything with anger, but this shit right here...brother, you're asking for trouble—if not death, then a prison sentence."

"And guess what? I don't give a fuck! I have nothing to live for anymore! My brother is locked up; Tamara left me after all we've been through; my mama and my family hate me; I need money; I'm sick of this shit called life! Just take this shit away man."

"Stop feeling sorry for yourself! And just do better..."

"You think it's that easy, pretty boy, huh? Huh!" I shove Nick into the side of the Escalade, ready to go one on one with him. I've had enough of his pep talks. "Let's go brah, you and me!" I pull up my pants and fold my fist.

"Kellz, I am not about to fight you!"

"Squad up! Fuck all this talking," I swing at Nick, but he dodges my swing.

"Kellz, stop it! I don't want to fight bro."

I aim lower and catch him in his stomach. He doubles over at the waist and gasps for air.

"Stop," he groans through the pain of having the air knocked out his lungs. "You're my brother. I don't want to fight you."

I ignore him as I go in for another hit. This time, Nick is ready and grabs me by my shirt and slams me forcefully into my car.

"I don't wanna fight you brah, but I ain't taking this shit no more. This is why Tamara left yo' dumb ass. You belong in jail since your miserable ass love to make everyone else around you miserable. You wanna stay in the streets? Well be my fuckin' guest, but don't try to take me down with you!" he yells.

I use my strength to push him off. "Some homeboy you are," I say, walking to the other side of my car.

"I'm a damn good homeboy. You just don't like to hear the truth."

"You're a bitch," I say back.

Nick opens the driver's door to the Escalade and hops in. "I swear if you would do better, your whole life would be so different."

He cranks up the car and drives off, leaving me in uproar. I can't believe my nigga would ditch me just because he a pussy-ass nigga.

Once again, I see the same black Dodge Charger with the same nigga hanging out the window. Only this time, the nigga makes a gun with his hands and points it straight at my face, pretending to shoot. The car then speeds off. I know what that means. I have to watch my back at all times.

I think about my brother. He would be the one I would turn to, if he wasn't locked up. While in the moment, I make the decision to visit my brother in jail. But right now, there's money to get and money to be made.

Chapter 21

TAMARA

I'm in the process of putting Tremaine to sleep when my cell phone begins to ring. I'm not surprised that it's Chauncey.

"Hello," I answer.

"Hey, babe. I got great news!"

"Yeah. And what's that, Chauncey?"

"Damn, babe. What's wrong?"

"Nothing. I'm just waiting for you tell me the news."

I'm quiet for a second until he decides to speak up. "Well, I talked to my dad about the waitress position at his restaurant, and he said that you can have it. It's all yours!"

I drop the phone on the bed. I don't know whether to cry tears of joy or scream. I shriek, "Oh my God! You have to be kidding me?" I pick up the phone and shriek again. "Oh thank you, C! Thank you, thank you, and thank you! This means so much to me!"

"Yeah. He said you can start next week. One of his customers booked for a celebratory party next Friday, and he said it's all yours. What do you say?"

"I say hell yeah!"

"Soooo," he says. "I would really like to see you. Are you busy?"

I giggle. "Nope. Come over. I just wanna hug you so tight."

He laughs. "I can't wait. See you in a bit."

After we hang up, I squeal. This time I wake Tremaine up, so I spend the next twenty minutes putting him back to sleep. I have to pinch myself to make sure that this is real. This is only one of my goals that I want to accomplish, and it's the biggest one yet. Now I can save money to get my son and me a place of our own. I can save money to get me a car also.

I will have the money to place my son in daycare when I go off to school instead of begging my neighbor to watch him. I will have money to take care of us both. Not depending on no man! When Chauncey finally arrives, I embrace him in a tight hug as I promised.

He smells of a rich cologne, and the plaid button-up shirt he's wearing compliments his caramel complexion.

"Come meet Tremaine, but be quiet. I just put him back to sleep." I lead Chauncey to my room that Tremaine and I share.

Chauncey peeks over the crib. "Awl. He's so cute and tiny."

"Yes, he is," I have to agree. "He was born premature, but he eats like a grown man." I smile as Chauncey chuckles.

"Because he's a boy. Duh, baby."

"Why you keep callin' me that?" I ask him playfully.

He shrugs. "Because I like to, but if it bothers you I can stop."

I shake my head. "No. It's better than shawty."

We both take a seat on the edge of my bed, and he grabs my hand. Every time he touches me, he gives me butterflies. It feels like a different touch. It seems sincere and caring instead of angry and rough.

"Thank you again."

He nods. "I told you I got you."

Silence fills the room for a while.

"Um, your face looks better," I say as I touch the side of his face.

"It feels better too." He does a nervous laugh.

Silence reigns supreme again. I lean over and begin to kiss his lips, and he returns my gesture. When we pull back, we just gaze at each other.

"You wanna try that again?" he asks.

We begin to kiss again, only this time with more passion and more hand movements as our tongues meet. He takes off my shirt and I take off his. This lasts until all of our clothes are on the floor, and I find myself sinking in the deep groove of our love.

After an hour or two of the most sensual, sweet lovemaking, we lie there in disbelief that this moment has finally happened.

"Wow," he says as I place my head on his chest.

"What? You didn't like it?"

He kisses me on my forehead. "Baby, I loved it."

"What does this all mean?" I say as I lean up to face him.

"It means...I officially want you to be my queen. On the real Tamara, I think I'm falling in love with you."

As he continues to talk, my mind flashbacks to the first time Kellz told me he loved me. Matter of fact, he told me while we were in the middle of an argument in ninth grade. We were arguing about something so stupid. We were freshman, and I wanted to show off my curves a little bit, so I wore these tight fitted-ass jeans that made my butt poke out twice as much. Then I wore a V-Neck shirt that played peek-a-boo with my bra.

Damn the attention I was getting! I mean, I had seniors trying to talk to me. I was young and not expecting to be in love, let alone have someone tell me that they were in love with me. I just wanted to be seen and liked by everyone. Anyways, Kellz saw the attention I was getting, and he freaked the fuck out.

"Tamara, don't ever pull this shit again, or I swear to God..."

"What?" I asked; he didn't say anything. "What Kellz?"

"I love you girl. Just don't pull no shit like this again."

From that moment on, I felt some type of way about him and our relationship. I saw that he was serious in pursuing me. Since that day, I made sure my jeans were fitted just enough and that my entire bra was covered.

"Tamara. Did you hear me?" I snap back to reality, and that guilty feeling rushes over my body again.

"Yeah. I heard you."

"So we can make it official? I just poured my heart out to you."

136

"Yes, Chauncey."

He smiles and leans over to embrace me. It doesn't register in my brain that I just agreed to jump into another relationship after I just got out of a four-year relationship.

"You just made me so happy," he says.

Suddenly the guilty feeling becomes greater. When Chauncey goes into the bathroom, I send Kellz a text saying *I love you always and forever.*

Chapter 22

ROXXI

Nick and I are shooting some hoops at the court today, playing a game of one on one. It's nice because we never really have time to do what we both love to do together as a couple. We play a couple more rounds until a gang of dudes want to hop on the court.

"Well, that was fun while it lasted," I say.

Nick nods his head in agreement. We grab each other's hand and walk towards the swing sets to get some alone time. It's Saturday, so I wonder why the park is so dead.

"I think Kellz is mad at me," he says with a worried look on his face.

"Why, bae?"

He sighs. "Long story. Basically, I spit some truth to him, and I refused to help him with his dirty work at his so-called job. I'm worried about him."

I shrug. "You know Kellz. He's a fighter. He'll eventually come around. Besides, Tamara still hasn't reached out to me yet."

Nick shakes his head. "They're just miserable."

"Yeah. Without each other."

"Hey Rox, I have been meaning to ask you if we could reschedule our plans tonight? Dad and mom want me to keep an eye on the brat. I hope you're not upset."

Of course I'm upset. I've been looking forward to this date since Monday, and now he wants to reschedule. "Yeah. I mean, that's fine. I guess." I stare down at the ground trying not to show too much disappointment.

"Awl baby. I'll make it up to you. I promise."

His words don't make me feel better. Okay, I may be making a big deal out of this, but we barely get to spend time alone, better yet go out on a date. We have always hung out with Tamara and Kellz or some other friends but never alone. And just when we make an official date, he cancels on me.

"I'll admit; I am a little disappointed. I was really looking forward to spending time with you and having our first date as an official couple."

Nick looks at me. "You're making me feel bad." He pouts out his lips.

"I'm sorry. I'm just being honest."

"I know, babe. That's why our next date has to be better than dinner and a movie because you are worth so much more than that. We need a weekend to get away. Just you and me."

I smile. "Really? You mean that?"

He nods. "Of course. Anything for my lady."

He kisses me on the lips, and I can feel myself cheering up. We look up as we see a shadow standing over us. It's a dark-skinned, bony guy who stands about five feet eight inches with dreads hanging to his shoulders. He's wearing an eye patch over his right eye, and his body is marked with all kinds of vulgar tattoos. He reeks of weed and looks as if he's lost several years of his life from using drugs.

"May we help you?" I say.

"Aye. You the light skin nigga that be hangin' around Kellz. Friend or nah?"

"Yeah. Who wants to know?"

The boy turns around and nods his head at a group of four dudes who are standing by the fence that surrounds the basketball court.

"Yeah, yeah. We don't fucks wit J-Money boys," the bony dude says.

"Who are you?" I chime in, but Nick touches my hand to signal me to keep quiet.

"Well that sounds personal," Nick says. The guys who are standing by the fence start to approach us. Nick looks at me and stands up. "Rox. Go home," he says as he stares at the group of guys.

"No! I'm not leaving you," I say as my heart begins to race. The guys just stand there, and I'm not sure what they're going to do next.

"That's yo' bitch?" the bony dude says.

"Watch your mouth!" Nick steps closer to the guy's face.

All of a sudden, the group of guys grab me, and I feel a blow to my stomach and a blow to the face. Then, I hear Nick shout as I fall to the ground. I see the bony guy pull out a gun on Nick, and I scream as the group of guys hold me down. "Nick! Don't shoot him! Stop!"

The guy freezes, looks at me, and points the gun at me. "Shut up, bitch!" he says. "Matter of fact, let her go!" When the guys let go of my arms and legs, he points the gun at Nick again and says, "Tell yo' fuck boy that he starting a game he won't be able to finish."

The guy pushes the gun in Nick's gut and pulls the trigger. I scream loud as hell.

"HELP!" I yell at the top of my lungs before I realize the gun didn't go off. The group of guys start laughing, and I damn near shit on myself.

"No bullets, fuck boy. Wipe that dumb look off your face. Make sure you give your boy that message because next time bullets will fly. And who knows...it may be you...it may be your bitch...it may be him...or all three of ya," he says as he walks off with his crew.

Nick helps me off the ground when the coast is clear and embraces me in a hug. "Rox, you straight?" I nod, still trying to digest what just happened. "We're going to get you home baby to clean your face, and I'm going to try to find Kellz."

"No, Nick. Please don't get involved!"

"If you didn't notice, I'm already involved. That crazy motherfucker just pulled a gun on me and threatened both of us. Our lives are on the line," Nick says.

"We should call the police then," I try to talk some sense into Nick.

"Then Kellz gets locked up. No, I'm not involving the police. Imma just go try to find him where we met at last night. Babe, I will be fine! Let's just get you home."

I shake my head and tears begin to roll down my face. I'm scared for our lives.

We ignore the onlookers on the basketball court as we walk by. I don't know how I'm going to explain this to my mom, so I'm just going straight to my room. I don't want to talk to anybody. I'm going to stay low—real low.

Chapter 23

NICKHOLAS

The date with Amaria wasn't going as I pictured it going. My mind is on my problem with Kellz, and I don't really speak much because I'm so busy blowing up his phone. He don't pick up not one time, and that causes me to worry even more.

I let Amaria in on what's going on, and she seems unbothered.

"Kellz is probably just busy," she tells me.

She really isn't paying me that much attention because she's distracted from all the attention she's getting from different men as they walk by our table. I'm annoyed. I mean, super annoyed with this chick, but I don't let it show. Besides, I can't feel any type of way; she's not my girl.

"I feel so famous," she says when she finally has flirted with all the niggas in the room.

I roll my eyes at her vainness. "I guess."

"Awl boo bear, don't be jealous," she grabs my chin and kisses it.

I smile. "Well, I want all your attention."

"As well as I."

But I can't give her my full attention. Not until I hear from Kellz.

Roxxi's blowing my phone up with text after text, but I don't respond. For one, I can't handle the guilt I feel for cancelling our date to take Amaria out, and for two, I have to stay focused. I don't want to seem suspicious.

After about fifteen more minutes of listening to Amaria ramble on about how famous she feels, I call Kellz again. This time, I am sent to voicemail. This nigga has been seeing me calling him this whole time!

I begin to get frustrated and mad. I shoot him a text asking where he is, but I never get a response. Finally, I decide to take matters into my own hands.

"Aye, let's ride out. I have to stop somewhere right quick," I say to Amaria.

After I pay for our food, I drive to the ratchet-ass strip club I met Kellz at the other day. When I pull up, the parking lot is deserted. Not a car or security guard in site. I get this eerie feeling in my body. Kellz can't be in here.

"Umm, Nick? Where the fuck are you taking me?" I hear the nervousness in Amaria's voice, and I definitely don't want to put her in danger, but I have to go check on my boy.

"It's cool, bae. Keep calm. I'll be right back..."

"No! You are not about to leave me in this damn car alone. I swear I will pull off in your shit if anyone walks up to it," she says.

I sigh. "It'll only be two seconds. I promise. Turn off the truck and lock the doors. I'll be right back."

146

Before she can utter another word, I slam the car door and head up to the building. Nobody is here and I wonder why. I still don't understand why my legs keep walking when my heart wants me to stop and turn back. When I walk inside, the place looks as if it has been ambushed by riots and angry people. There are chairs, trash, and bullets all on the floor.

"Where the fuck is the police? Why aren't they here?" I say as I look at the destruction to the building. I start walking to the back towards J-Money's office. I have to figure out what the hell happened here...and if Kellz was caught in the crossfire.

When I step inside the office, it is trashed. I look around for evidence, but I just find more bullets. Someone has had a field day. I walk towards the desk, then suddenly step back when I notice the two security guards face down covered in blood. But no J-Money.

Oh my fuckin' God! Should I call the police? I think as my phone starts to vibrate. It's Amaria. "Hello," I answer.

"Get your ass out of there! A car full of niggas just pulled up, and they look like trouble. Meet me around the street. Hurry!"

I race for the door so fast I don't even feel my legs moving. As soon as I run outside, a bunch of niggas hop out of this black Charger loaded with guns. "Get his ass!" one yells.

Oh shit! I run across the parking lot, praying that the bullets they're shooting miss me. Please God, don't let me die this way! I race between an alleyway as I still hear gun shots, but none of the niggas is behind me. I think I lost them for a sec, so I hide behind a dumpster and quickly dial Amaria.

"Where are you?" I shout. "My fuckin' life is on the line!"

"I'm at the gas station up the street. I had to get out of sight."

I look down the alleyway and see a couple shadows. The niggas must've split up looking for me. Fuck!

"Aye, fuck boy! Where ya' hidin'," one of them calls out.

Okay Nick, I tell myself. *Just run for it. Get to the gas station. You can do it. It's just right up the street.*

I take a couple deep breaths and begin to run again. I make sure I'm hidden in dark spots and that none of the guys are following me. I run and run and run. My legs don't stop until I hop in the truck, and I yell for her to pull off.

"Oh my gosh, Nick! What the fuck?" Amaria cries when I jump in the car. "This is the craziest fuckin' date I ever been on!"

I shake my head. "I'm...sorry," I manage to say in between breaths.

She laughs. "OMG babe. I just got an adrenaline rush!" She kisses me on the cheek.

"What was that for?" I ask, confused.

"You don't understand. Guys like you turn me on. You didn't tell me you were such a bad boy." She kisses my cheek again. "I haven't had such a rush since the strip club I used to work at was raided by a bunch of gang bangers who wanted my ex-boss murdered—executional style. Literally, they stopped the show and made everyone watch as they cut his damn head off. It was horrific. Then, they turned themselves in afterwards. They gave no fucks!"

I sit up in the chair and try to take in all the information she just spilled. Strip club...gang bangers...beheadings...? Did shit like that excite her? Was this bitch fuckin' nuts?

"Ummm," is the only thing that manages to come out of my mouth.

"I know, I know. I sound crazy. But I grew up in the country, and when I moved to the city I had never experienced most of the shit city girls have experienced. I only seen shit like that on TV. So that was wild."

"Well, most people never witness a person getting their head cut off. That's not normal," I say with a smirk. "But you used to be a stripper?" I ask.

She nods. "Yup. My folks moved to Atlanta when I was 18. After I graduated, my home girl talked me into exotic dancing. I started off at a small strip club in Atlanta, but as I got more popular, I moved to Strokers. By twenty, I had stripped at about five different clubs, some in Atlanta and some in Augusta, then I met the love of my life—well he used to be—and we got married—."

"Married? Are you still married?"

"Chill daddy. We were only married for about eight months until I learned he was controlling and was cheating on me with multiple women. We divorced like four months ago."

"Four months ago?" I retort again. She looks at me and cringes. But hell, I should be the one cringing. The more she talks the more I learn about her, and I'm not sure I like what I'm hearing.

"Yes. Is that a problem?" I say nothing. "Look Nick, if you're going to play around and judge me then I don't think we need to talk. My life was crazy, so you tell me if you can handle the baggage. Tell me right now."

I stare out the window. In all honesty, I have too much shit on my mind right now. Minutes ago, niggas I don't even know was trying to end my life.

I look at Amaria, and I just want to fuck. She has too much going on for me to try to be in a relationship with her. She's a bad girl, but something about her turns me on. I mean, look at her. She is a trophy and every nigga wants her, but I'm the only one who had her. That makes me not only a man—but THE man.

I turn to look her into her face and say, "I got you baby girl. No judgement this way."

When we get back to the crib, she leans over to embrace me in a tongue-filled kiss. I want her so bad. Shit, maybe being inside her will take my mind off my problems.

"I really like you, Nick," she says in between our breaths.

"I really like you too. So why don't you show me how much you like me?"

She pulls back and smiles. "I would love to, but my parents are probably still awake, and plus I have to keep you guessing." She winks.

For real, I ain't want to guess. I can tell it's good by the way it sits up in her shorts...her pussy is phat! "Damn, after all we been through tonight, you still gon' make a nigga wait?"

She nods. "If I'm worth it, you'll wait."

I nod. "Yeah, I can agree with that."

We end our crazy-filled night with a good night kiss, and we go our separate ways. I attempt to call Kellz once more, but there's still no answer. Finally, I respond back to Roxxi's texts and the guilt rushes over me.

Fuck! Fuck! Fuck! What am I getting myself into?

Chapter 24

KELLZ

I see Nick blowing up my line the whole time, but I ain't want to talk to his ass. I'm still pissed at the way he came at me the other day. I thought he was my boy, but I guess he's turning his back on me, just like everyone else.

I spent the last couple nights at Sha'tila's apartment but reminded myself not to get too comfortable—although I am. She treat a nigga like a KING. She cooks a nigga breakfast every morning and makes dinner every night. She treats a nigga to some good sex. She rub a nigga feet and massage my back. She showers me with affection and laughs, and we puff on the best gas that I smoked in a long time.

For the past two days, we stayed in the crib getting to know each other. Of course, I told her about the Tamara situation. I told her how I felt about it and how bad I wanted these feelings to go away. She told me about her past boyfriend who used her and set her up just to steal money from her.

I mean for real, shawty is banking. She drives a costumed pink 2015 Ford Mustang sitting on pretty rims. Her apartment, which is in the uppity part of town, is decked out with expensive furniture. Her closet is decked out with red bottoms and clothes a nigga can't afford to buy his girl—at least not yet.

Later, I found out she is big on saving. She has been working since she was sixteen, plus she owns her own online business as well as does hair, nails, eyelashes, eyebrows, and all that other fake shit bitches get as a side hustle.

I'll admit a nigga is impressed. Too impressed. Shawty is all about her money, and a nigga loves that about her. I'm starting to think she is out of my league. She told me that a lot of men are afraid of her independence, so her relationships never work out.

I tell her that it doesn't bother me, and, as a matter of fact, her drive turns me on. She feels relieved about that. I guess that's her way of tellin' me she's feelin' me.

My phone starts to vibrate again. Nick's calling my phone.

"Damn, shouldn't he be studying for his graduation test? Or running behind Roxxi? Why the fuck is he worried about me? He has other shit he needs to be focused on," I say to Sha'tila who's lying next to me in bed.

"Just answer, Kellz," Sha'tila says.

I sigh and give in. "Yeah," I answer.

"Do you have any fuckin' idea what I've been through? I've been trying to call you, and I know you seen me calling. Where are you?"

"Laying low."

"Well, there is trouble!"

"Yea, like what?" I ask nonchalantly.

"I went looking for you at the strip club, and I saw that somebody shot up the club. Bullets were everywhere and both of the security guards were dead, and I couldn't find J-Money. I didn't know whether to call the police or what. Then, this car full of thugs were shooting at me as I was running for my life. I mean—"

I sit up in the bed. Now he has my attention. Those thugs must've had something to do with the strip club being shot up. They're hiding something. And where was J-Money?

"Wait. What kind of car was it?" I ask.

"Black Charger," he answers. Just then, I get a flash back of the nigga hanging out the window of the same exact car, imitating shooting a gun at me.

"Fuck! That's the same car that rode past me a couple times before!"

"Yeah, and don't let me mention the gang of niggas that pulled a gun out on me and Roxxi at the park, and they were looking for you!"

"What?" I yell, becoming infuriated. These fuck niggas have no need to bring my friends in this bullshit.

"What? What's wrong, boo?" Sha'tila asks tugging on my shirt.

"Actions has to be taken," I say, ignoring her.

"Are you crazy, Kellz? These goons are looking to kill us. Graduation is in two weeks, and I am not trying to die," Nick says.

"I'm not askin' you to roll wit me, but they ain't bout to threaten my peoples. Fuck that. I got something for they ass. I know just about where they hang out spot is."

"Kellz...come on bro—"

"Please save yo' pep talk. These niggas askin' for it."

"Kellz—"

"Shut up, Nick."

"I'm coming with you. I'll meet you at the club."

I become quiet because I'm thrown off by his words. "Nawl. You don't have to. I know how you feel about this shit."

"Nawl, I got your back. Meet in thirty?"

"Aiight."

When I hang up, Sha'tila's is bursting with curiosity. I let her in on the situation, and of course she doesn't want me to go over that way starting trouble. I don't give a fuck. When she realizes that I'm not going to change my mind, she wants to come with me.

"Noooo, I can't let that happen," I say.

"Come on, boo. I will be fine."

After minutes of her begin', I give in. "Fine. Let's ride..."

Chapter 25

NICKHOLAS

I pull the truck next to Kellz's car, and I take a deep breath. "Dear God," I pray, "Please keep us protected. Please don't let me die before I walk across that stage. In Jesus name. Amen."

There's a tap on my window, and I notice Sha'tila standing by Kellz's side. "Sha'tila?" I question as I open the car door. "What are you doing here?"

"She's rolling with us. I know how you feel about guns, but you might want to hold on to this." Kellz hands me a nine millimeter semiautomatic pistol, and this time I take it.

As we approach these run-down shotgun houses that look as if no one has stayed in them for years, my stomach begins to churn. I know it's too late to back down now, but I can feel my heart pounding in my stomach. I'm not diggin' the vibe of this place at all.

"It has to be one of these houses I saw ol' buddy come out of. They hang over here somewhere," Kellz says, leading us further down the street.

We notice a group of niggas hanging on the side of one of the houses.

157

"This is it," Kellz says approaching the crowd of niggas. One of the guys starts whistling while the other guys are making provocative comments towards Sha'tila.

"Damn girl, all that ass. What's up with you?"

As soon as one of them tries to grab her, Kellz loses his shits. "Keep your got damn hands to yourself!"

"Or what?" one of the niggas asks.

"Imma kick your ass, that's what," Kellz retorts back.

"Boo, let's just go," Sha'tila says, reaching for his arm.

"Better listen to her, fuck boy," another one of them says.

"You don't want no problems." Kellz steps up to the main nigga's face.

"Only problems I have is one of you fuck boys messin' with my peoples. You mess with them, then you mess with me!"

The group of niggas laugh in harmony, and I can see that it irritates Kellz even more.

"Kellz, let's just get out of here. Obviously they are taking this as a joke," Sha'tila says.

Kellz falls quiet. "Sha'tila, go back to the car."

"What? Why?"

"Just go," Kellz orders. As she walks away, Kellz turns his attention back to the crew and, before I know it, Kellz throws a punch at the one who's talking shit. Next thing I know, a brawl breaks out. I'm getting blows to the head, chest, arms, face, and stomach. All I can see is arms and fists flying everywhere. As I finish fighting off one nigga, another nigga comes to throw punches. My breath is becoming short, and my head feels light. I can't handle fighting off another nigga, so I have to think of something and fast!

"Don't nobody fuckin' move!" I hold the semiautomatic towards the gang of niggas, thankful that the brawl is over.

I didn't think my plan through though, 'cause I don't know what to do next. Kellz follows my lead and pulls out his piece. My head and my body are exhausted and pounding with pain. I don't want to start anymore trouble. I just want to get the hell up out of here.

"What yawl gonna do with those?" one of the thugs says, taking out a gun of his own. "It's our guns against your guns. You bitches are outnumbered."

I look at Kellz and motion for him to put his weapon down. As I tuck the gun back in my jeans, I can taste the blood in my mouth. We're outnumbered, and there isn't shit we can do. Kellz thought he was going to solve the problem but only made himself look like a fool by approaching all these niggas. And here I am looking like a fool right beside him.

I don't know how I'm going to explain my face to my parents. They're going to freak the fuck out. Suddenly, we hear a car horn, and everyone turns to look.

"Come on you guys," Sha'tila yells to us. "I just saw a couple cops heading this way. We need to go now!"

The thugs begin to run and scatter. "Fuck! It's twelve," one of them yells before hopping over the fence into the backyard.

"Come on, Kellz!"

Kellz and I rush to the car.

"Hey, what about my dad's truck?" I ask, looking out the back window as she pulls off.

"We're goin' to go back and get it. Don't worry. I just needed to get you guys out of there. You guys look horrible. What happened?"

"This ass started a fight he knew we couldn't finish," I say. "I thought you had some kind of plan for sneaking the niggas," I say, looking at Kellz.

"Fuck you," Kellz says. "I still kicked ass. I don't know about you, homeboy."

I roll my eyes because obviously Kellz doesn't understand the gravity of the situation we're in.

"Okay guys. Just chill. The important thing is you guys are okay." Sha'tila kisses Kellz on the cheek, and my mind begins to wonder about how deep their relationship is getting.

I hope, for Kellz's sake, that she isn't crazy like Amaria...Oh yeah...Amaria. I check my phone to find a couple messages from both her and Roxxi. I have a message from my dad asking me if I was safe and telling me that I better be making it home right now. He sent that thirty minutes ago. Fuck! I need to clean myself up.

"Hey. Do you have anywhere I can go to clean myself up before I head home?"

"Of course," Sha'tila said. "That's not a problem."

After we pick up my truck and I clean myself up to the best of my ability, Kellz hands me a clean shirt and tells me to let him know when I make it home. Sha'tila tells me to be safe.

"Watch your back out there, Nick," Kellz says as I walk out, and his words send chills down my arms. I'm not the enemy. He is. But I'm tangled in this bullshit nonetheless.

I'm already an hour and a half late, so I know I'm going to get the shitty end of the stick when I get home. I open the front door waiting for my parents to be standing there getting ready to let loose the rapture of screams. I look around downstairs. No one is there. I think I've gotten away with it, but as soon as I open my room door, my mom appears in the hallway. "Nick. Baby, where were you?"

"Uh, I was just out and about, ma," I reply, still facing my room door. I can't let her see my face.

"Are you okay?" she asks as I can hear her footsteps coming closer.

"Yeah, ma. I just want to go to bed. Have another test tomorrow."

She touches my shoulder to turn me around and then lets out a loud shriek. "Honey," she yells. "Come look at Nick's face! Nick, oh my God! What happened? Baby are you ok?" Tears flow out of her eyes, and she touches my face.

"Nick? What's going on, son?" my father asks, entering the overly dramatic scene caused by my mother. I even see Devon peeking out of his room door.

"Nothing for you guys to worry about. I'm fine."

"Boy, you have three seconds to tell me what happened to your damn face!" my father says. "One..."

I open my mouth to explain and then stop because how the hell would I explain this fucked up situation to my parents?

"Nick," my mom pleads again.

"Two..." my dad continues to count, and I feel my face becoming hot with embarrassment. "Three..."

"Okay! Kellz and I got into a fight with this gang of dudes! And the guys pulled guns out on us; the cops were coming and we dipped!"

Smack!

That's the sound of dad's hand going across my face. My face is really red now.

"Honey. Calm down!"

"What did I tell you boy? Kellz ain't nothing but trouble! Now look at your got damn face! You want to walk across that stage..." dad paused. "That's if I decide to let you walk across that stage."

"What?" I ask stepping up to his face.

"Boy, you better back the hell up!"

"You can't stop me from walking across the stage."

"Like hell I can! You disobey my house, then you will suffer my consequences."

"Hell no! I will leave this bitch before you stop me from walking."

Another smack to the face. "That's strike two," dad yells.

"Stop slappin' me," I yell back. "Damn!"

I enter my room then slam the door on their faces. I'm heated. I'll be damned if he stops me from going to graduation. Not after all my hard fuckin' work. I can't fathom what just happened. I begin to feel lightheaded again, and the last thing I remember is blacking out.

Chapter 26

TAMARA

I awake feeling confident about the English test all seniors have this morning. English will be a breeze. I'm surprised that Tremaine isn't crying or at least making noises, so I rush over to his crib to check on him. My heart jumps when I notice that his crib is empty. I run to my sister's room, but it's empty too. Then, I hear Tremaine's giggles coming from the kitchen. I go into the kitchen and find him in my mother's arms, and she's playing with him. I close my eyes and reopen them. I step a little closer to grab for him, but she brushes me off.

"It's okay, Tamara. He's fine."

I glance at my mother and cringe when I see her face. Both of her eyes are black and the right one looks like it has been through war with her man's fist. Her eyes are just as puffy as her swollen lips. She has cuts and scrapes on her cheeks and hand prints around her neck.

"What happened to you?" I ask.

She starts to weep. "He tried to kill me, Tamara. He nearly choked me to death. Not to mention the burns from his cigarettes all over my body. I'm in so much pain."

I grab Tremaine so she can get a hold of herself. I hope she doesn't expect me to feel sorry for her. She abandoned us for two years messing with this guy, and now his true colors are exposed to her. I'm sorry she's in pain but not sorry that he beat her. I tried to warn her about him, but she never listened. Those nights I cried that I was hungry, she never listened. Those nights I needed someone to confide in, she was never there. When Tremaine and I was about to be living in the dark. She was never there. Kellz was.

Suddenly, my heart sinks, and reality begins to wash over me. That's why I don't need to jump into another relationship. I still have feelings for Kellz. I mean, Chauncey is a great guy, but I don't want to break his heart by still being in love with my ex. I have to call it off with Chauncey.

"I'm dropping Tremaine off at the babysitter. I'll deal with you later," I say to my mother.

"No! I'll watch him. Let him stay with me."

"Hell no! I don't trust you with my baby. Besides, you need to get yourself cleaned up and to the hospital. And just maybe you need to lock his ass up for good," I say as I turn to walk away. She grabs me, but I snatch her hand away. "Don't touch me."

"Tamara, I need your help. I'm so sorry, baby. Please, I want to be here for my girls and my grandson." She starts to wrap her arms around my leg as she gets on her knees begging for my forgiveness. I don't have time for this shit.

"Get off of me!"

"Tamara please. I'm begging you. I'm done with him; I promise. Please let me be here for you."

Tears begin to well up in my eyes, and my chest becomes heavy. Tremaine starts yelling on top of her begging, which adds fire to the flame. My scream quiets the room until Tremaine begins to cry.

"Let go of me. I have to go to school."

She looks at the ground as if she is ashamed of her begging. She unwraps her arms from my legs. To win me over, she has to do more than beg.

I rush to get Tremaine ready to go to the babysitter so I won't be late for my test. After I drop him off, I briskly pace myself to class. I think about Chauncey as I walk through the school doors, so I send him a quick message telling him we need to talk. He agrees to meet with me after school.

I feel good about the English test. When we have our lunch break, Roxxi sits beside me to see how things are going. I lie and tell her things are okay when deep down my whole world is in pieces.

I put my pride aside, and I apologize to her, and then we catch up on a few things. She tells me about what happened at the park, and instantly I know Kellz is in some type of trouble. I have to check on him. I tell Roxxi about my job, but I leave out the incident I encountered with my mom this morning.

I just don't feel like the conversation taking that route. After school, I meet up with Chauncey by his car, and he embraces me in a warm hug. Maybe before I would have appreciated the gesture, but now I wish that it was Kellz's arms that were embracing me.

"What's up, babe? How did your test go?"

"Um...great actually. You?"

"Well, you know we aced it." He chuckles.

"Of course we did," I agree.

"So what's on my beautiful queen's mind?" He smiles at me, and my heart sinks to my chest.

OMG, I can't be doing this all over again. I give him a nervous smile in return. It becomes quiet.

"Is it about Kellz? This relationship? Or are you pregnant?" he says playfully. "If you're pregnant, then I'm excited." He laughs at himself then halts when he notices my straight face.

"No, I'm not pregnant, Chauncey. I've been thinking..."

"What have you been thinking about?" The smile suddenly leaves his face, and a serious look enters his eyes.

"That maybe we should continue building our friendship, I mean it's..."

"You're not over Kellz. It's going to take some time. Blah. Blah. Blah."

"Don't mock me!"

"You're not telling me anything new, Tamara. Damn! How long is this shit going to take? I thought you wanted a change. I thought you wanted a man not a nigga. What about all that shit you told me you've been through with that thug nigga? And please, don't tell me you didn't want to hurt my feelings."

"Well, I'm sorry! I didn't expect us to turn this into something. Is that the only reason why you wanted to help me, Chauncey?" I ask.

166

"No," he denied, "but don't you dare try and flip this shit around on me. You're the one who is lost. I know who and what I want."

"Uuuggghhh!" I bury my face into my hands, attempting to stop the tears from flowing.

Naturally, I look for his comfort, like always, but when I don't feel his arms embracing me, I look up. He doesn't even attempt to break the silence between us. He just stands there, arms folded, staring ahead with this angry but hurt expression on his face.

"Chauncey, just give it time. Give me time. Give us time, baby," I say, finally breaking the silence.

"Fine," he says snapping back to our conversation. "We'll give it time. However much time you need." His response is chilling, maybe because it's the way he said it.

"Please don't be mad at me, C. I'm trying."

He shrugs. "It's all good. We can remain friends. And the job is still yours, and I'm still here if you need me. We're cool?"

I nod. He glances at me one last time before he hops in his car and drives off. I can't believe his reaction and the fact that I'm single.

Chapter 27

KELLZ

I sit at the table waiting for the officers to bring my brother in for our visitation. In my head, I'm contemplating the things I should say. I don't know if I should tell him that I'm in some trouble or not. If I tell him, what could he do about it? He's already in jail because of my stupidity, ignorance, and dumb mistake.

My legs start shaking, and my palms become sweaty. I haven't visited him in a while, and I haven't wrote him in forever. I have no stable home. I've been between Mr. Charles' and Sha'tila's crib for the past week. So if he wrote me, more than likely he sent the mail to our mother's address, and I haven't been over there in months. Knowing her, she probably threw those letters away because she still has hatred in her heart towards Terrell when I'm the one she should be hating.

Five minutes pass when an officer shows up with Terrell. My brother looks different. He has guns of steel. His beard has grown down to his chest, and he has a couple of gray hair strands in his mini afro. His eyes look tired and distraught, and he looks as if he hasn't ate in months.

"I'm surprised to see you here, brother," he says as he sits across from me.

"Yeah, I see you been working out," I chuckle to lighten up the mood, but Terrell doesn't budge.

"How come I haven't heard from you? You let me down. You're the only fam I have, and you've been MIA."

I stare at the table. Not only did he hit a nerve, but that's the same shit I spit to Tamara, and here I am neglecting my own brother.

"I'm sorry, bro. I just been going through some things, but that's no excuse," I manned up and admitted.

"How's mom?" he asks.

I shrug. "Good I guess. She kicked me out a few months ago."

"Drugs?"

I nod affirmatively.

"Where have you been stayin'?"

"I've been back and forth between Mr. Charles' crib and this girl I'm talking to."

He squints his eyes. "New girl?"

"Yup. Tamara found her a new guy. Apparently, he's more charming than I am. He makes her happy."

"Wow," he replies, and it gets quiet for a moment. "You stayin' outta trouble?"

I shrug. "Sort of."

"What does that mean?"

"Hey look," I say, hoping to change the subject. "I know somebody who can get you outta here. All I have to do is work for him."

My brother slumps back in the chair and folds his arms. "Is that right? I'm listening."

"He says he can pull some strings. He knows people. Brah, wouldn't that be dope? I mean, I got you into this mess, and Imma get you out."

Terrell just stares at me, and his vibe is slick irritating the fuck outta me. He just has the same blank expression on his face. Does he not have love for me anymore? He is quiet for a sec as he stares at the ground.

"You know what I heard?" he asks, glaring at me. "I heard that you in trouble wit them Eastman boys. I heard they lookin' for you. I heard you working for Jim. The same fuck boy that got your life on the line right now." He pauses. "Know what else I heard? You the talk of the streets. 'Cause niggas who work for J-Money attract enemies. Why the fuck you think nobody works for his ass now? This is not his set! He came here and fucked with the wrong city, Kellz. I heard about the strip club getting' shot up. J-Money is missing. Where's your nigga now? Either dead or they shipped his ass back to Mississippi where he came from." He pauses again. "I'm so disappointed in you. All I wanted was for you to get off these streets. You're my baby bro, and I love you more than anything. I swear I don't want to see you in a casket!"

His eyes begin to well up with tears, and my memory flashes back to the scene of my brother being emotional while being placed in the police car and the time when they convicted him of murder during his court trial; tears fell from his eyes then too. I've never shed so many tears and neither has he. I was depressed damn near a year before my heart began to fill with rage. But what and who was I mad at? Myself!

My brother and I was so close. We spent every day together. He was the one who woke me up every day for school and told me to be somebody. He sat there and made me do my homework. He told me I should be the right man for Tamara. He told me to always respect my mother and my peers. Never to let a nigga see me sweat and stay smart—both book and street smart. He told me to face every challenge on my feet.

But I let him down. I let him down years ago. The moment I pulled that trigger, I let him down. This should be me in these ugly-ass orange suits. This should be me with the bags under my eyes and gray hair poking out of my head. I wonder if it was me, would Terrell have changed his life around. Would he be married with kids? A business owner? Would he and ma dukes be the best of friends? Would he have a college degree?

I feel the pain rising in my chest as I fight back the tears. I can't let him see me break down. I have to be strong for my big brother. We all we got.

"My worst fear," he says in between sobs, "is me losing you to this fuck shit. It's nothing in these streets, Kellz. I promise you. Niggas talk too much. I gotta watch my back because niggas know you my brother, and they think you a sellout. I'm trying to hold it all together, but I don't know how long I can take this shit."

"Stop talkin' like that," I yell as tears stream down my face. "You're gonna be fine! We're gonna be fine! Imma get you outta here! Just please...please stop talkin' like that."

I feel like a pussy for letting my emotions get the best of me, but my brother is talkin' about killin' himself. Then who would I have?

We both sit there with our emotions running wild. My brother never seen me cry even when I got whoopins as a kid; I never shed a tear. Pain is something I'm very familiar with. When my pops left, I was four, and my brother was eight. That's when I experienced pain for the first time.

Pops was everything to us. He made ma dukes happy, at least we thought, but when he fucked around and got injured at his job, which caused him to be out of work for a while, mom slept with another man. He caught her dead in her tracks. We had to stop him from beating her ass. A month later, he was gone.

We never felt sorry for our mom. Instead, we held so much anger towards her for the longest. From there, we stayed with our grandparents for a while until mom got her shit together. We shared a small-ass room, sleeping on bunk beds with broke-down mattresses.

Our grandparents were very strict. Every day after school, we finished our homework and had to play outside. Dinner began at 8 p.m. promptly; we could watch TV for an hour, then it was off to bed.

Finally, we got tired of the bullshit, and we became rebellious. It wasn't long before our grandparents shipped us back to our mother. From that point on, we didn't give a fuck about life or anyone. All we had was each other. And because of our bond, I'm shedding these tears.

"Don't worry about me, bro. Just get yourself together," he says.

"Rell, there is no me without you. I promise you; I'm going to get you out of here."

"But you don't even know where that lil' fucker is."

"I'll find out. I got this."

"Okay, time is up guys," the officer says.

Terrell just nods.

"Just hang in there."

"Promise you'll get off these streets, Kellz. Please."

I nod as we embrace each other in a brotherly hug. "I got you, brah."

When I walk out of that jailhouse, I make it my duty to find J-Money so I can get my brother out of here. But for now, I have to lay low.

Chapter 28

TAMARA

Testing is over, and the results are in! The past couple weeks have been crazy, but I can proudly say that I am a graduating senior along with my fellow friends. Not only that, but I love my new job; mom has started cooking dinner and looking for a job and being friends with Chauncey isn't so bad after all.

Graduation is this Friday, and I feel so relieved that it's all over. I've been in such a jovial mood that I have been texting Kellz, and he agreed to meet up at my house today. I want to personally invite him to the graduation and give him this gift I've been holding for a couple weeks now. I bought him a gold necklace with a *T* on it while I bought one with a *K* on it for myself.

I look in the mirror to make sure the new outfit I bought is straight. I have a pair of black jean shorts on with rips in the thigh section and a peach halter top that brings out the color of my skin. I decide to let my dreads hang because recently I dyed them purple, and I'm digging the new look. It's bold. And there was a time I would never go for a bold look. Today, I'm feeling myself all too well.

175

My stomach fills with butterflies when I hear a loud knock at the door. I'm glad Tremaine is gone with my mom. I had to set my pride aside to trust her with him, but I told her to be back in an hour. She is just supposed to walk him and take him to the park for a while.

I open the door and smile. Kellz's appearance is different. Well, maybe that's because I haven't seen him in a while, but he looks too good. He's wearing a pair of black jeans and a black tee shirt with a gray bucket hat to match his gray Jordans.

"You trying to dress like me?" I say, making hint of his black jeans.

He chuckles. "Nah. I just jumped fresh this morning. I like the new look though."

We embrace each other in a hug, and I motion for him to come in. I'm not going to lie, it's a little awkward because I don't know what to say to him. "You seem different," I say, taking a spot on the couch next to him.

"Yeah. How is that?"

I shrug. "I don't know."

"Good or bad?"

"Good...how you been?"

"Good. You?"

"Great. I have a job now."

"What? That's what's up! Congratulations. Where at?"

"New restaurant downtown." I make sure not to mention that it's owned by Chauncey's dad.

"Coo'. You like it?" he asks as he sits back on the sofa.

"Yes. The tips are amazing."

176

"Where's Tremaine?" he asks, smiling.

"Out with ma. Her and her boyfriend broke up, so she is back trying to make everything better." I roll my eyes at that thought.

"Good. That's what you've always wanted right?"

I shrug. "Yeah, it's going to take some getting used to though." I walked to my room to grab the necklaces and handed the box to Kellz. "So, I got you something," I say as I hand it to him.

"What's this for?" He looks at me and smiles.

"Just because you're amazing. Open it."

As he opens his box, I open mine, and I'm relieved when his smile gets bigger. "T?"

"Yeah a T for Tamara, and I have a K for Kellz. You like it?"

He chuckles. "I love it. It's dope."

I lean over to wrap my arms around his neck, but instead our lips meet for a kiss. It feels like when we first met. Maybe that's what I was noticing about him. Maybe that is what I'm feeling. The butterflies, the urge to embrace him in hugs, and the burst of sensation as we lock lips.

He lays me down on the couch as I proceed to take his shirt off. The kisses become heavier and more seductive. I haven't felt like this in a long time, and I'm caught in Kellz's web of fire. I bask in the wonderful feelings coursing through my entire body.

My lungs become heated as my heart yearns for every touch. My stomach warms as the butterflies turn into fireflies, and my legs begin to shake as he gifts my neck with kisses. I don't want this moment...our reunion...to end.

He starts to take off my top, but there's an unexpected knock on the door. A knock that extinguishes the beautiful fire we made.

"You better get that," he says, lifting me off the couch.

"Ugh..." I say, nodding. I make my way to the door and freeze when I open it. There's Chauncey standing at the door with roses and a card. "Wh-what are you doing here?" I whisper.

"T, I just came by to say that I don't want us to be friends. I want us to go back to being more. Babe, I promise you, you won't regret it."

"Chauncey," I start to speak but he cuts me off.

"Tamara, please take me back."

Suddenly, Chauncey's face drops when a shirtless Kellz appears at the door.

"Damn, T. So you both were exclusive?"

I shake my head. "No, Kellz! It wasn't like that—I..."

"What was it then?" Chauncey chimes in. "Were you just using me?"

I turn to Chauncey. "No Chauncey, I didn't mean it that way."

I turn back to Kellz who seems stunned by the whole situation. Then, he starts to laugh. "Ah man, this shit is so funny. You invite me over here, give me a gift, and we're about to handle our business until this clown comes over here whining, and now you entertaining his ass?" he says to me with questions in his eyes. "Don't mind me, Chauncey. Imma let you get back to begging, my nigga," he says to Chauncey as he starts to put on his shirt.

"What was going on here?" Chauncey asks me.

"Nothing."

"Why is he here then? I thought you two stopped talking?"

"We did, but..."

"But what?"

"I'm sorry, Chauncey," I say looking at the ground. I really didn't know what else to say to either of them. I'm so fuckin' embarrassed.

"Were you trying to get back with him?" Chauncey asks, but I don't answer him.

Kellz sighs. "Well, I'll holla atcha later T. Maybe we can pick up where we left off another time."

Tears begin to flow down my eyes. "Wait, Kellz. I don't want you to leave," I say to his back as he walks down the street and gets into his car.

Chauncey just stands there looking at me. He is hurt. I can read it on his face.

"Were you going to have sex with him, Tamara? Just be honest."

I'm unsure whether I should tell him the truth or just tell him that my intentions were just to give him the necklace and invite him to graduation. It was either full truth or half-truth. "Maybe," I finally say.

Chauncey smacks his teeth. "So you ain't shit either?"

Immediately, my mouth drops open, and it takes everything in my power to not smack the shit out of him. "Don't say that," I yell.

"It's true!" Next thing I know, I have a bouquet of roses thrown at my face and card pieces shriveled at my feet. "Thanks for showing me your true colors, Tamara." He turns to walk off before turning to me once again. "And from now on, you can find your own damn ride to work!"

And just like that, my nightmare begins all over again. I swear I can never be happy. I can never wake up with a smile on my face without being followed by drama. I hate my fuckin' life so much. I'm always stuck in the middle of bullshit.

I didn't want to hurt Chauncey, but at the same time I never intended to hurt Kellz. All I could do was lie in bed and cry. Endless sobs and endless sorrow. That is the story of my life.

Chapter 29

KELLZ

It's Friday: the day of all my friends' graduation, and I'm on my way to support their accomplishment. The graduation starts in nearly an hour, but I decide to make a last minute stop. Of course, it's supposed to be my day too, but a nigga has been prohibited from walking across that stage. I was told that I need eight credits to pass, as well as a passing grade in all of the graduation tests, but I made it up in my mind that I'm done with school. If later on down the road I want to finish, I'll just go back to get my GED. But I know that there are ways to make money without having a diploma or degrees.

Mr. Charles is very disappointed in me. All day, every day, he would nag about how important education is and why I should consider staying in school. Finally, I had heard enough of his bullshit. I packed up whatever belongings I had over there and left.

Sha'tila told me that I could stay with her until I get back on my feet. A nigga is forever grateful for that, but it has me wondering where the hell we're taking this "relationship" between us. So far, all we've been doing is fuckin', but she shows her feelings by cooking for me or just planting kisses on my lips every five minutes. I mean, I'm diggin' it, but I ain't in no rush or nun. I'll just go with the flow.

Standing in the store, I stare down at the bouquet of flowers I picked out for Tamara then contemplate whether or not I want to give them to her 'cause shawty was buggin'. She tried to play my ass again with the fuckery, and we ain't even together. I ain't feel no type of way about the nigga beggin' and bitchin', but I feel like she slick tried to set me up. After that whole scene, she kept callin' and textin' me nonstop until I gave in and spoke to her ass. And when I went back to her house to pick up where we left off, she let me know just why I'm standing here with these beautiful flowers in my hand.

The flowers are a mixture of green, pink, yellow, and blue flowers. I contemplate giving her something more than flowers, but I say fuck it. I don't want to look like no pussy. Maybe Chauncey will shower her ass with more shit. I just don't want to show up empty handed.

My mind begins to flash back on all the memories we had. Those talks she wanted to have about our future. She wanted us to be married by the age of twenty-five, and she wanted five kids. She had dreams of us both being career oriented living in this beautiful two-story home in the country. The way she described it and the details she provided always sent chills down my spine. She was that good.

She knew exactly what she wanted outta life and how she wanted our life to be. She would always ask me did I plan to be in the streets forever, but I never had an answer. I mean, the streets is all I know. I have no clue what working a nine to five is like. It can't be that fun.

I refuse to work for the white man. I rather have my own business, and, to be honest, that is my dream. If I can't accomplish that, then I will forever be in the streets. And the thing about owning my own business is I don't need a damn high school diploma to accomplish it.

I purchase the flowers and head straight for my car. I don't know what it is, but I can't shake this feeling I have in the pit of my stomach. I can't describe it either.

Chapter 30

TAMARA

All of the graduating seniors stand around with jitters and excessive energy. It is almost like everybody had at least five cups of coffee today. My palms are sweating due to the nervousness in the pit of my stomach. Don't get me wrong, I'm hella excited and ready to grab for that diploma.

Roxxi and I gift each other with hugs every ten minutes. I'm happy for my best friend and vice versa. I didn't think I was going to make it to this day with her.

Nick is clowning with the other guys doing what guys do. They even spark up one last roasting session before everyone parts ways, not only for the summer, but for the rest of our lives.

I could feel a tear stream down my cheek 'cause I also didn't think I would do this being single. Kellz and I had plans to graduate together ever since we became acquainted with each other. Although he told me he doesn't care about school, he made a promise to me that he would finish.

The only reason he passed the classes he did was because people did the work for him. He actually paid students to do his work. I remember the time I had an English paper due. It had to be at least ten pages, and it was to be formatted MLA style.

He paid Chavon Jefferson, the school's highest scholar, two hundred bucks to do my paper. He told me he did it so we could spend time together. That weekend, we went out to the movies, shopped at the mall, bought ice cream, and went laser tagging and everything. I ended up receiving an A plus on my paper, and Mrs. Halt used it as an example work.

I smile, reminiscing about the old times Kellz and I had. I miss those times, and I want them back. I ruined everything and for what? Kellz is my soul mate. My partner. My best friend. My homie. My lover. And I sacrificed all that for nothing.

I snap out of my feelings. I tell myself that I am okay. I will make everything right, and I am happy. At this very moment, I can say I am okay. My mother is here with Tremaine; I have a job; I started applying for colleges, and I am ready to become that person I have always envisioned myself to be.

Chauncey is still upset with me. He hasn't uttered one word to me since that big scene at my house. But today, I don't let it bother me. My mind shifts back to Kellz, and I am hoping he is going to make it. He promised me he would. That will mean the world to me. If he doesn't make it, I will surely be hurt. Maybe I deserve it though. After all, I did hurt him.

I've never seen him so upset. The only time I've seen him cry is when his brother got locked up, and that shit hurt me to my heart. I take out my cell phone to give him a call, but there is no answer.

Graduation is about to start soon, but it's just like him to be late. I wait another five minutes and dial his phone again. Still no answer. I can't worry about it anymore because we have to start lining up.

A few seconds later, my phone vibrates, notifying me that I have a text message. It's from Kellz letting me know that he is on his way. I smile and let out a breath of relief.

Chapter 31

KELLZ

Folks wanted to drive all slow since I'm in a hurry. "Come on people! I have to go see my people graduate, fuck!" I see that Tamara called me, but I'm too busy trying not to hit these slow-ass drivers on the road. I honk my horn at the dumb-ass driver in front of me who sits for three seconds when the light turns green. They honk back and I honk again. "Fuck you!"

My only choice is to hit the highway, if I want to get there on time. I hit a shortcut so I can bypass the traffic jam at the traffic light and take the back way through the hood towards the highway. I guess everybody is trying to make it to graduation. As I speed down the neighborhood, I notice this gray '96 Chevy Impala racing up behind me.

"What the hell?" I say aloud as the car rams into the back of my car.

My car and body jerk forward, and my head meets the top of the steering wheel. Next thing I feel is another bump into the back of my car, and this time my head jerks to the side crashing into the driver's window. Again another ram until my car completely stops in the middle of the road.

I try to yell for help, but I'm too shocked to do so. Quickly, I reach for my phone to text Tamara, but I can't find it. I search for my Glock, but forget I left it at Sha'tila's crib as I left in a rush. I'm in a panic as my head pounds with pain. So many thoughts go through my head. I don't want to die. Not now.

My vision is going in and out, and I can see the blood dripping from my forehead. I proceed to open up the car door and crawl my way out the car.

"Hey, somebody help me!" My voice isn't loud enough. "HELP!" This time it's louder, but no one is in plain sight. The houses are almost deserted, and the street is empty.

Suddenly, a tall, slim figure dressed in all black appears in front of my face, and my whole body goes numb when I get a glimpse of him. "What the fuck?"

"What the fuck?" He laughs devilishly. "Surprise my nigga. You shoulda known one day somebody would catch your ass," he says as I try to stand up. He kicks me to the ground again. "You ain't going nowhere. I hope you know I have to make this quick. Yo' boy J-Money is next. Nobody likes a traitor, Kellz. I thought you were with us homie? Guess you did it for the money, huh? Can't spend money when you're dead, K. Hood. It just doesn't work that way."

At that very moment, I feel betrayed. This is someone I trusted, but he was one of them on the low. "Fuck you," I manage to say as I start to choke on the blood in my mouth.

He points his gun towards me. "That's cool—"

Suddenly, I find the strength to grab for his legs, knocking him down to the ground. "Get off me nigga," he yells.

We both wrestle for the gun. Ain't no way in hell I'm going to die without putting up a fight. I throw a couple punches to his face, hoping he would lose his grip on the gun.

"You fuckin' low-down muthafucka!" I say just before he throws a punch to my head, resulting in me losing consciousness. Tamara's beautiful smile along with the glimmer of hope in my brother's eyes when I told him I would leave the streets alone, flash before my eyes. Then shots are fired, and I go out like a light.

To be continued...

NEWSLETTER SIGNUP

Thanks for your support! To receive future updates from Shani Greene-Dowdell Presents, text NAYBERRY to 22828.

More Reads from Shani Greene-Dowdell Presents

Noelle's Rock: A BWWM Holiday Romance

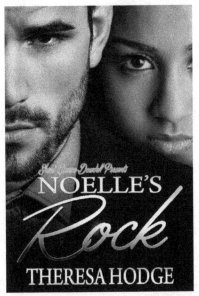

Side Piece Chronicles: A Durty South Love Story

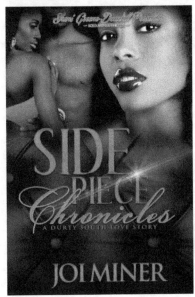

CPSIA information can be obtained
at www.ICGtesting.com
Printed in the USA
LVHW031918211019
634872LV00013B/366/P